The Young Prince and His Fate

The Young Prince and His Fate

Jessica Wheeler

To order additional copies of this book, contact:
Xlibris
1-888-795-4274
www.Xlibris.com
Orders@Xlibris.com
815238

Chapter 1

With fate, there comes a sacrifice. You learn what your future is without finding out for yourself first. There was once an old tale of the fate-rose. It looked like any normal rose, red with a green stem. There was something incredibly special about that rose. It gave people the power to see what their fate was before they could find out for themselves. The rose, however, came with consequences. Those who seek the rose to find out their fate soon fall into a deep sleep for about three days. When they awake from the slumber, everything appears normal as they have no memory of the rose; but soon, the victim will begin to become weaker and weaker until they can no longer walk and are put on bed rest.

Eventually, their bodies will fade away because of having no more energy left in them. No one knew what the cure was to the fate-rose. When cases of them happened, people sought help from the enchantress, Elenor. Even she could not figure it out as the victims had dropped dead before she could get the chance to find it. Because of the number of deaths caused by the fate-rose and for everyone's safety, Elenor used her magic to banish the rose from all the land of the kingdom of Monrock so nobody could find it again. After the banishment, no one has seemed to find it. It stayed that way for a long time, but soon, everything changed when it happened again for the first time in one hundred years to a boy who was the next heir to the throne.

The kingdom of Monrock. It was a huge kingdom, and everyone

had their place where they belonged. The kingdom was ruled by King Mangus and Queen Regina, who met when they were kids. Mangus was the heir to his father's throne and took over when he was twenty-one years old. Mangus and Regina were shortly married after becoming king. The kingdom adored Mangus and Regina. They both deeply cared for their people and would do anything to protect them. When they roamed on the outside of their castle, everyone always stopped to greet them.

The citizens loved their king and queen. They had two children, a daughter named Reya and a son named Ranvir, who were five years apart. They were excited as the kingdom has never had a girl as an heir to a throne before. However, things took a turn for the worst. On the way back home from another kingdom's wedding, a storm approached. The storm destroyed their ship, killing Regina and Reya in the process.

Mangus grieved for months over the loss of his wife and daughter while running the kingdom and taking care of Ranvir, who survived. Ranvir was incredibly young when it happened and did not quite understand why his mother and sister suddenly just disappeared. Mangus knew he would need to have a heart-to-heart conversation with his son to tell him the truth. When Ranvir turned five, he kept constantly asking about his mom and sister, mainly when they were coming home. One particular night, Ranvir came down into the kitchen to get some water, where he found his father sitting in front of the family portrait in tears.

"Daddy?" Ranvir said.

Mangus looked over to see Ranvir out of bed and quickly wiped away his tears.

"Ranvir. You gave me a fright there, son. Why are you out of bed? You should be asleep," Mangus said.

"I just wanted some water. Are you crying, Daddy?"

Mangus scoffed and gestured for his son to come to him. Ranvir ran toward his father, and Mangus held him close.

"Is that Mommy and Reya?" Ranvir said.

"Yes, son. This portrait was actually taken when you were just a baby. Our family was complete," Mangus said.

"When are they going to return, Daddy? It's been too long."

Mangus knew he needed to tell Ranvir the truth. He knew it would hurt his son to know the truth, but he needed to tell him.

"Look, son. Do you remember the time when I told you about your grandfather Mangus III?"

"Yes."

"And where did I tell you he was now?"

"Up in the sky and through the stars."

"That's right. Anyway, well, Mommy and Reya have joined your grandfather. After that horrible storm, your grandfather knew they were no longer safe here on earth, so he took them with him."

"But when is he going to bring him back?"

"That is the point, Ranvir. Mommy and Reya are not coming back, bud. Not anytime soon. I'm really sorry."

Ranvir did not know how to take the news, so he started to cry onto his father's shoulders. Mangus rubbed his back and kissed his head.

"Why are they never coming back, Daddy?" Ranvir sobbed.

"I wish I knew, bud, but everything always happens for a reason," Mangus said.

"I want them here." He sobbed.

"I know you do. I do too. We all want them back here with us. But one day, you will see them again. You can always look up to the sky and stars like you always do for Grandpa. Just know that you are my biggest reason why I have gotten through the pain. I see your mother and sister through you. I know you'll make a great king one day."

"What if I could never be a good king like you?"

He held his son even closer. Mangus knew he needed to be the one to give him the reassurance as Regina was the one to do so with him when they were kids.

"Ranvir, a good king does not appear overnight. You are only five. In fifteen more years, with good practice, you will be ready. You just have to believe in yourself. I can already see you as the king."

"Really?"

"Really. Take a look. All the heirs lined up in a row here in this picture. When you become king, your picture will be added. At least the tradition will keep going. Your sister was originally going to break it being the first girl, but now it will be you. I will teach you everything there is to know about being king, Ranvir. It's you and me against the world now."

"You promise, Daddy?"

"Cross my heart. Nothing will come between us my son. I promise."

They hugged tight. Ranvir felt better now hearing that he always had his dad despite losing his mom and sister. Mangus finally felt relieved after telling Ranvir the truth. He thought it went better than expected.

"All right, to bed with you now," Mangus said.

"Race you up there," Ranvir said.

Mangus playfully chased Ranvir up the stairs and put him to bed. He closed his door and walked toward the portrait of the family before the shipwreck.

"Things are hard without you, Regina, but don't you worry. I will make sure to do whatever it takes to make our son the best king of Monrock," said Mangus.

Chapter 2

By the time Ranvir was ten, Mangus did everything in his power to teach his son everything there was to know about becoming a proper king. After losing his wife and daughter, he became very protective toward Ranvir as he started to fear losing him as well.

"Rise up, Ranvir! A king is always up early," Mangus said.

"Ugh! Dad, just one day. Why can't I sleep for one day?" Ranvir said.

"Ah, but you're learning to become a king. To learn, you must start to act like one. First things first, a king is always up early to start the day with his people."

He got Ranvir out of bed and made sure he was paying attention throughout the entire day. Ranvir was only ten years old, and all he wanted to do was play with his friends, but he knew that he had to learn how to be a king when his turn comes.

"Second, you must always interact with your people. The relationship between the king and your people is extremely important, son. These are your people you are going to be looking after your entire life, so it is important to always make a great first impression. Try it. Smile and wave, son."

Ranvir smiled and waved at a few people. Mangus was very embarrassed by his posture.

"Posture, son. Stand up straight. Shoulders down."

Ranvir rolled his eyes and did what his father asked him to do.

"Third, always be confident in yourself. If you aren't, then your people won't be either. It is always important to lead by example."

"But I thought a king has to lead by pride."

"Yes, but when you make your choices, you need to be confident in yourself. Sure, maybe your people will disagree with you, but as long as you feel confident in your choice, that's all that matters."

"I think I had enough king practice for today. Can I go now?"

"No, son. Your friends can wait until later. Your people always come first! Friends should always be your second priority, because who comes first?"

"Our people."

"Correct."

"But how did you make time for Mom and us?"

"Well . . . it is hard sometimes, but she and I always found a way to make the best of our time when I became king. When you and Reya came along, it was easier. People were more understanding because we have kids. It is not easy running an entire kingdom by yourself. It is not. After your mom passed away, it all sank in that I would have to do it all on my own. It was hard, but at the end of the day, I had a kingdom to take care of, and, most importantly, I had you. It takes a strong person to step up to the plate to handle two important things in their life. Your mother and sister would be so proud of me right now for pulling through."

"Will I have to run the kingdom by myself?"

"I don't know, son, but you don't have to worry about it now. You still have a long road ahead of you before you become king. I am sure you will find someone before you become king. I will say it is easier to have a queen by your side, but at the end of the day, you have a kingdom to take care of. Relationships should also be a secondary part of your life."

After more lessons throughout the day, Ranvir was finally allowed to hang out with his friends. He always enjoyed those days where he did not have to act like a king and could be his normal self. He immediately met up with his friend Cecila, whom he has been friends with since he was six years old.

"Hey, Ranvir," Cecila said.

"Hey."

"Another fun day of learning to be king?"

"I guess you can say that."

"Wanna go to the river under the bridge? We can look for frogs."

"Boy, do I! My dad cannot know about it. He would have a heart attack if he knew that the prince was playing with frogs."

"He never lets you be a real kid, huh?"

"Well, I mean, sometimes, but he wants me to start acting like king material. I understand where he's coming from, but there are times where I wish he would allow me to be a normal kid for a couple of days."

They walked down the river together. Ranvir always had Cecila to talk and rant to. He knew that he could talk to her about anything, and she was always there to hear him out.

"Watch your step here. It's easy to fall."

"I haven't been on this side of the kingdom in ages."

"Well, now you can get a glimpse of it. Soak it all in while you can."

They started to look for frogs. Ranvir was very careful not to get his clothes wet as Mangus would get mad if he knew his son was out looking for frogs. Cecila eventually found one and tried to splash him with water.

"Whoa, careful! My dad can't know that I am out here, remember?"

"Right, sorry."

They walked toward the bridge and sat quietly. They stared out into the sunset. Ranvir always liked looking at the sunsets because he would forget about being a prince for a second to just enjoy something so small.

"So how are you feeling about all this?" Cecila asked.

"I mean, it's all right, since I'll have to deal with it when it becomes my time. I'm sure I'll have a different mind-set when I get older."

"I know you were only young when it happened, but do you have any memory of what happened to your mom and sister?"

"Well, I mean, not really. I don't even remember the shipwreck. All I remember is that one day, my mom and sister were there, and one day they weren't. My dad told me the truth eventually, and that's when I realized they were not coming back."

"Where do you think your life would be if they still were alive?"

"I don't know. One thing for sure is that I would not be training to become king. My sister would be getting the training to become queen instead of me. But, honestly, I feel like I would not have it any other way. I feel like I would still get some type of special training in case something happened to my sister, whether she would not be ready or simply just leaving royalty forever. Again, I don't know where it would have led to if she was still here. I really don't know."

"Well, at least your dad is doing the right thing."

"I know."

"You'll be a great king. Like you said, your mind-set will change, and I'm sure you'll be more positive about it."

"I hope so. I would hate to see my dad disappointed if I didn't want to become king."

"Ranvir! Where are you!" Mangus shouted.

"I need to go. See you after practice tomorrow?" Ranvir said.

"You know where to find me."

Ranvir quickly ran back to the castle. He lost track of time and ended up being late for dinner.

"Ranvir, where were you?"

"I was with Cecila. I'm sorry I lost track of time."

"There is no excuse for being late as a king. A king must always be on time. No excuses."

"I'm sorry. It won't happen again."

"I sure hope not. That's embarrassing on my part having a son who can't be on time."

"I said I was sorry."

"Sorry doesn't cut it, Ranvir. Get that through your head. If you want to be a good king, then you need to start taking what I'm saying more seriously. If you don't start now, then you will never be by the time your coming of age comes around."

"I'll try harder next time."

"Not try, you will!"

"Yes, Dad."

"Eat your dinner now. It's already starting to get cold. That wouldn't have happened if you were home on time."

"I said I was sorry, though."

"Like I said, Ranvir, sorry doesn't always cut it. A king must always take responsibility for his actions."

Ranvir started to eat his dinner. Mangus scoffed seeing Ranvir not keeping his posture.

"Ranvir, sit up. Napkin in your lap. Chew with your mouth closed."

"Sorry, Dad."

"What did I say about being sorry?"

"It doesn't cut it. I get it!"

"Lower your voice. We are at the dinner table, not at a joust."

"I just want to eat dinner in peace."

"Well, if you would just follow the simplest stuff, I wouldn't have to keep getting on you all the time."

"I'm just a kid, Dad."

"My kid! The prince! The next king!"

Ranvir slowly ate his dinner trying not to make eye contact with his father. He loved his dad, but sometimes he wished that his father would cut him some slack. Ranvir sometimes thought about if his sister was still here that he wouldn't be getting critiqued every five seconds and wouldn't have his dad cramping stuff down his throat. Although he had those thoughts, he knew that he was the heir to the throne and had to accept his responsibilities as the future king.

Chapter 3

Ranvir was now twenty years old. He was only a year away before his coming of age. A lot has happened through the past ten years. He had a girlfriend named Agatha, whom he dated for six years. They met at one of the royal balls the kingdom throws every year. Ranvir was not much of a dancer, but he knew if he was going to be king one day, he needed to mingle with other people. Also, his father made him socialize with people that night, and he wanted him not to hang out with Cecila, as he wanted him to talk to other people. He found her sitting all by herself, and his instincts knew to go over and talk to her.

"Sitting all by yourself, huh?" Ranvir said.

"Well, I don't have a choice when I don't know anyone," Agatha said.

"Well, I'm Ranvir, the prince of Monrock. Now you know one person."

She laughed. "Yeah, I guess so."

"So did you just move into the kingdom?"

"I did actually, so I don't know anyone except my parents, siblings, and you."

"Well, welcome. I'm glad you took the courage to come out here tonight. It takes a strong person to do so."

"Yeah, my parents wanted me to get out of my comfort zone."

"Well, like I said, it takes a special person to do so."

"So what's a prince like you doing over here talking to me?"

"I mean, you were sitting here all by yourself. Plus, my dad makes me socialize with people too, especially since I'm next in line to be king."

"That's good! Do you feel ready?"

"Well, I can't say for sure that I am, but my mind-set changes every year, so I'll probably have an answer for you then."

"I hope so. So, basically, the people in the kingdom gave us the background on you and your dad. I'm deeply sorry to hear what happened to your mom and sister."

"It's OK. It happened when I was two years old. I honestly don't remember it. I just remember that, suddenly, they were gone. But, yeah, my sister would have been the heir to the throne if she didn't die, but, apparently, there is a reason for everything."

"Well, I'm sure you'll make a great king."

Ranvir smiled. Just then, a slow song came on. It suddenly became a little awkward. Ranvir ceased the courage to ask Agatha to dance with him.

"Well, everyone is dancing. Shall we go join them?" Ranvir asked.

"Are you asking me to dance?" Agatha asked.

"Only if you want to. No pressure."

"Sure, I'd love to."

"All right."

They both went up to the dance floor. Mangus smiled seeing his son socialize and dance with a girl.

"That's my boy!" Mangus said.

Both Ranvir and Agatha felt a little awkward dancing together, since they just met for the first time. Eventually, they started to ease their way into the dance and became comfortable with each other. After the ball ended, the two started to hang out frequently each day. Ranvir started to develop feelings toward her. He wanted to tell her but was scared of what her reaction was going to be. On another day of hanging out, Ranvir was thinking about it and could not get his thoughts off his mind. He knew he needed to tell her.

"Agatha, I really need to tell you something."

"Sure. What is it?"

"Well, ever since I met you at the ball that night, you've constantly been on my mind. I really like you a lot. I felt that connection when we first met. I really want you to be my girlfriend, but if you don't, I totally understand."

"Ranvir, I feel the same way about you too! Of course, I'll be your girlfriend."

Ranvir was overcome with joy. He finally got his first girlfriend. Throughout the six years they were together, everything was going great. Soon after they hit six years, however, their relationship took a toll.

Agatha was going through a hard time. Her dad had passed away, and she was having to help her mom raise her younger brothers. She felt like she couldn't get any time for herself. As much as she didn't want to, she was leaving the kingdom to be on her own. Ranvir didn't take the news very well, especially that he was planning to propose to her.

Ranvir waited for her in the flower garden, as that was their usual hangout. Ranvir felt the hair on the back of his neck stand up. He was extremely nervous. He lightened up when he saw Agatha, but he soon frowned seeing her upset.

"Agatha, is everything OK?"

"Not really, Ranvir. Everything has been so stressful this past year with my dad dying and me having to be a caretaker to my brothers. I just don't have any time for me anymore. This just isn't what I want anymore. I don't want to be locked inside a kingdom all my life. I just want to be free. I made the decision that I'm leaving Monrock for a while to clear my head."

Ranvir was blindsided by her response. He did not expect anything like that out of her. He felt his heart tear open into a million pieces.

"So you're just leaving?" Ranvir asked.

"I'm sorry, Ranvir. I love you so much, but I just need to clear my head for a while. It's not you. It's all me."

"Agatha, please don't do this to me. After everything we've been through, you really just want to throw it all down the drain?"

"No, but I just need time to myself. I will be back for you. I promise."

"Are you sure?"

"I promise, Ranvir. I will come back, but not any time soon. Give me a month, and I promise I will come back."

They shared a hug. Ranvir could no longer hold back his tears. He knew he had to let Agatha go for only a short period. He had faith that she would come back.

"I will come back. You just have to trust me," Agatha said.

He held her hand. "I trust you," Ranvir said.

He led her to the gates. They kissed each other good-bye. Agatha got on her horse and rode off. Ranvir watched her ride away. He grabbed for the ring in his pocket and held it close. What was supposed to be a wonderful moment turned into a heartbreaking one. He kept saying to himself that she would be back, but, sadly, she never came back. A month turned into two months, two turned into three, and now it was a whole year and Agatha never came back for him.

Ranvir stood outside of the castle in ponder, thinking of Agatha. The more he thought about her, the more his heart hurt. After going through his heartbreak, he realized that he might have to become king without a queen for a while. Seeing his father run the kingdom by himself was tough enough, and it made him stress out knowing that he might have to go through that. Ranvir was now more hesitant than ever to become king.

"Still thinking about Agatha?" Cecila asked.

"Yeah. She hasn't left my mind since she first left," Ranvir said.

"I'm still confused why she would do that to you."

"I wish I could too, but, sadly, I don't. She hasn't even bothered to write me a letter or anything. Why did I put my trust and faith into her if this is what she was going to do?"

"Well, you know how some girls are. Honestly, you deserve an explanation from her."

"Indeed, I do. I have even tried to write to her a few times, and nothing. What's the point of trying more if I'm not going to get anything back anyway?"

"I hate to say it, Ranvir, but the fact that she hasn't come back for you and that it's been a year strongly implies that it's over."

"It can't be."

Ranvir started to cry. For a girl whom he loved dearly, she completely left him in the dust. The fact that he couldn't even know why hurt him even more.

"Ranvir, I know it hurts, but you'll be all right. I promise. It will just take time."

"I know."

"I'm always here if you need anything. You know that."

"Thanks, Cecila."

"Anytime. Do not let her actions define you. Keep being you."

Ranvir took the time to collect his thoughts and put everything behind him. He went up to his room and came across the ring in one of his drawers. The memory of that horrible day kept popping into his head.

He tried so hard to block out that memory. The more he tried, the more hesitant he was about becoming the next king of Monrock.

Ranvir made his way down to the dining hall to eat dinner. Mangus knew that his son was still upset about Agatha. He went through the same pain when Regina died.

"Look, son, I understand your pain."

"I really loved her, Dad."

"I know. I liked her a lot too. I know exactly how you feel. When your mother passed away, I felt like the inside of me tore open. But as much as it hurt, I had a kingdom to run and you to take care of. The pain eventually wore off once I distracted myself. Things will get better for you eventually."

"I don't know, Dad. Honestly, I don't think I'll be ready to become king next year. I don't think I'll be capable of being king on my own."

"Well, about that . . ."

"What?"

"Son, I know you've been going through a hard time right now, but I was thinking about it for a long time now, and I think it's for the best that you become king now. I think your coming of age should be as soon as possible."

"WHAT!"

"I think it'll get your mind off Agatha."

"And I suppose that I'm just supposed to listen to you!"

"Lower your voice, Ranvir. There is no reason for you to be raising your voice and getting upset."

"I HAVE EVERY RIGHT TO BE GETTING UPSET!"

"Ranvir, this is a part of what I trained you for all your life. You knew it was coming. I don't know what has gotten into you all of a sudden. I know you're still hurting, but that is no reason to be backing out of your heir. You need to do what is right."

"I'm not ready to be a king on my own without a queen. I'm not going to go through with this coming-of-age thing! You can't make me! You won't!"

"Ranvir! Ranvir, don't you dare walk out while I'm talking to you!"

Ranvir stormed out of the room and slammed the door behind him. He went straight up to his room and cried his eyes out. He was nowhere ready to take on such a huge responsibility all by himself. After seeing his dad have to do it alone, he knew that was not what he wanted. He heard a knock at his door.

"Ranvir, I need you to really think about this. It's about stepping up to the plate and taking your place. Please let me in. Let's talk about this."

Ranvir didn't want to talk to his father, but he knew that he would find a way in one way or another, so he just decided to let him in.

"Ranvir, I don't know what has gotten into you, but that was totally unacceptable what you did back at the dinner table."

"Well, how can I control my emotions when you're moving my coronation up early?"

"I just think becoming the king now is what's best for you."

"To do what? Stress myself out and not having anyone to rely on like what you had to go through? I'm not capable of doing this on my own. Not without someone to rule with me. I honestly didn't know who I was without Agatha."

"Ranvir, you don't need a queen to rule a kingdom. Get that out of your head. I know you are worried, but nobody said it was easy. The task of a king doesn't just happen overnight. It takes time. You just need to rebuild that confidence that we've been talking about."

"I'm sorry, Dad. I just don't think I want to do this without a queen. I can't."

Mangus didn't know what else to say to Ranvir. He felt like everything he was saying to him was going in one ear out the other. He let his son be and walked to one of the family portraits. He put his hand on it. Although Mangus raised Ranvir alone, he sometimes didn't know how to get through to his son.

"If there was time I wish you could be here, Regina, it would be now. If only you were here, he would have listened to you."

Ranvir continued to mope in his room. He looked at another blank sheet of paper and started to go back and forth on whether he should write another letter to Agatha. He was stuck on what to do. He could either try again and face the fact he would not get anything back from her, or not write the letter and not get anything back. Ranvir didn't want to risk feeling more hurt, so he did not go through with writing another letter.

Why? he thought. *Why did this have to happen to me?*

Chapter 4

Days passed, and Ranvir was still hesitant about becoming king. Throughout the time when he was growing up, he would constantly see his dad stress out having to do it alone. After Agatha left, he knew that he did not want to live in his father's footsteps and run a kingdom all by himself. Although his dad and the people of the kingdom have told him that he does not need a queen to help rule, he was oblivious toward their comments because he claimed that they aren't the ones who have to go through it.

"Ranvir, rise up!" Mangus said.

"Ugh. Just leave me here!" Ranvir shouted.

"You know the drill, Ranvir. A king—"

"Is up early! Yes, I know. Blah, blah, blah. I'm not becoming king, so there's no point in getting up this early anymore."

"Not the case, Ranvir. You will not be an embarrassment as long as I am king. Now get up. We're holding another ball tonight."

"Oh, please, Dad. Don't make me go to another one! You know going to one is just going to tear me apart even more."

"Ranvir, I know you're still hurting, but you are the prince! You need to be there. Who knows, you might even meet another girl there. Then you'll get your motivation to become king again."

"I don't think it works like that."

"Well, which is? You act like you don't want to become king without a queen, so it couldn't hurt to try and talk to other girls, and Cecila does not count. Or you can stop acting selfish and just become king like you're supposed to."

"Fine! I'll talk to other girls."

"Start getting ready."

"But the ball isn't until tonight."

"Correct, but it looks like you haven't gotten out of bed in weeks. Start getting ready now. No son of mine is going out there looking like that."

Mangus walked out of the room. He was beyond frustrated with Ranvir. He thought he was being very selfish by not wanting to become king all because he didn't have a queen. To give his son the motivation he needed, he talked with the other kings in other kingdoms who would be attending the ball about representing their daughters for an arranged marriage. He knew Ranvir wouldn't be happy, but he knew that Ranvir forced it upon himself for being stubborn about becoming king.

As Ranvir got ready for the night, he was still processing the fact that he would have to move on from Agatha. He was not at all ready to do so, but he knew Cecila was right about the chances of her coming back were very slim. As much as he didn't want to believe it was over, he faced the music and told himself that Agatha was never coming back. There was a knock on his door.

"It's open," Ranvir said.

Cecila walked in. She knew that Ranvir was going through a hard time and ceased the opportunity to be there for him.

"Hey. Are you OK?" Cecila asked.

"My dad told me that I needed to look for someone else at the ball tonight."

"But, Ranvir, do you really think you need a queen to solve everything there is to becoming king?"

"I saw my dad struggle and stress out at times after my mom died, Cecila. I can't follow in his footsteps."

"But do you really think finding another girl is going to solve the problem?"

"Apparently. Agatha is not coming back. That's very clear."

"Just because Agatha decided to leave doesn't mean that you don't have what it takes to become king."

"I'm not trying to be rude, Cecila, but you aren't becoming queen, so you don't know the stress I am going through."

"Yes, I do. I have been your best friend since we were six. I've watched your pain and seen you stress, so don't sit there and say I don't know what you're going through! I just wish you could just listen to what everyone is trying to tell you."

"I have to continue getting ready. I'll catch up with you later."

Cecila felt frustrated with Ranvir. He was so stubborn and oblivious to what everyone was trying to tell him. She saw no point of trying to help him if all he was going to do was shut her down.

"Ranvir, are you almost ready?" Mangus asked.

"As ready as I'll ever be."

"Stand up straight. You know how your posture should be."

"Well, I can't help the fact that I'm actually going to try and move on from Agatha. We've been to every ball together."

"Just keep your head up and smile."

They walked down to the ballroom. Ranvir had more butterflies in his stomach. When they opened the door, he saw a lot of girls compared to all the other times. He got a strange feeling about it. He did his best to mingle with some girls, but Agatha kept appearing in his head.

"King Mangus, I present my daughter Angelica for your son," one king said.

"I present my daughter Caroline," another said.

Ranvir couldn't help but notice that Mangus was talking to other kings and their daughters. A sudden thought appeared in his mind. Was his dad trying to set him up with another girl? Ranvir was outraged and made a beeline straight for him.

"The game is over, Dad!"

"Huh? What do you mean?"

"I know exactly what you're trying to do! Stop acting like you don't know what I'm talking about."

"Son, come walk with me."

He gently grabbed Ranvir by the arm. "Son, I'm only trying to do what you want."

"And that is what?"

"To give you a queen."

"So what are you saying?"

"All right. You may have guessed correctly. I'm trying to do an arranged marriage."

"YOU'RE TRYING TO DO WHAT!"

The room went quiet. "Ranvir, lower your voice!"

"Are you crazy? You're trying to set me up with a girl I don't even know and marry her. I can't believe you, Dad!"

Ranvir was very livid. He stormed out of the ballroom. Mangus chased after him. Out of all the years of being king, he had never felt more embarrassed in his life.

"Ranvir! Stop this behavior this instant!"

"No! I'm so tired of you getting on my back about this whole being-king thing. You're making it all about yourself!"

"What are you talking about?"

"You're trying to give me an arranged marriage. That's not the life I want."

"I hate to say it, Ranvir, but you are acting like a child right now. You're being so stubborn about becoming king. You refuse to become one unless you have a queen. You literally gave me no choice but to try and give you an arranged marriage."

"That doesn't mean I wanted one! It's your fault for wanting me to become king early! This is all about what you want! Did you even bother to ask me what I wanted? No! I'm tired of you bossing me around and trying to make my decisions for me! Why can't you just get through your head that I don't want to be king! I don't want to be like you! I don't want to go through the stress that you went through not having a queen by your side! I don't want to be you! I don't wanna act like you! I WISH THAT IT WAS ME THAT DIED INSTEAD OF MY SISTER!" Ranvir raged.

Mangus was blindsided by everything that Ranvir said. He couldn't even help but shed a few tears after hearing that his son would rather be dead than be king. Mangus had no words to say to his son. He didn't know what to say.

"Ranvir, I'm running out of options for you. You tell me you don't want to be king without a queen. I go out and try to find you one, and this is how you're going to talk to me. I'm sorry you're still hurting, but you have got to stop rehashing your past. But this is what I have been preparing you for your entire life. I'm sorry, but I cannot turn back time and prevent that shipwreck from happening and having your sister being the queen. It doesn't work that way, I'm afraid. You have a choice. You can become the king without a queen, or you can do the arranged marriage or even attempt to find Agatha to become the king. If I'm being honest, you are more than capable of being the king without a queen. I know you're tired of hearing it, but it's clear that you're not going to listen to anyone. I'm done with trying to help you. It's time that you made a decision. Sadly, I cannot make the decision for you, as this is your life. Your choice has to come from you. Be careful with which one you choose."

Mangus walked away, discouraged that he and his son are failing to see eye to eye. He felt like a failure thinking that he couldn't do anything more to help his son become king. There were times he wished Regina could be here to help with that, but he knew that Ranvir needed to come to his senses and do what was right for himself and the kingdom.

"Ugh! What is it going to take for my dad to realize that I don't want to become king!" Ranvir shouted.

He started to throw things in his room and shout at the top of his lungs. Ranvir was very outraged at that point. He felt like a monster was growing inside him. As he was throwing stuff in his room, he came across a book that he never opened.

"What the heck? How did this get back here?" Ranvir said.

It was the legends of Monrock. His dad gave him the book as a gift a long time ago on his thirteenth birthday but never opened it. There was a reason why he never opened the book.

"Happy birthday, Ranvir! I can't believe you're thirteen already. It feels just like yesterday when you came into this world. You were so handsome! I remember your mother crying when she first held you. She truly loved you with all her heart. At least she was here for two of your birthdays rather than none at all," Mangus said.

"I remember those two birthdays! I'd do anything to see her smile again. I'd also do anything to hug my sister again," Ranvir said.

"I know, son, but they are always with you. Never forget that."

"I know, Dad."

"I know you opened your gift already, but I have something else for you. It's from your mother. She said not to give it to you until your thirteenth birthday."

He gave him the gift. He opened it slowly to reveal that it was a book on the legends of Monrock.

"Hmm, interesting."

"Yeah. She wanted you to get familiar with the background of Monrock when you became King Reya."

Ranvir paused for a moment and looked straight at his father. "You called me Reya."

Mangus froze knowing that he accidentally called Ranvir his sister's name as he knew that the book was meant for Reya and not for Ranvir. He couldn't get any words out.

"This book was never meant to be given to me, was it?! It was for Reya, wasn't it?"

Magus couldn't even look at his son. He knew he messed up big time at that moment and didn't know how to fix it.

"Mom never meant to give this to me! Why would you lie to me!"

Ranvir started to cry. Mangus held him close. "Son, I'm sorry. I just thought that she would want you to have it now that you are the heir."

"But the fact it wasn't made for me is what really hurts. I don't feel special anymore."

"Don't talk like that, Ranvir. You are special. If your mother was here right now, she would want you to have this book. She would be so proud to see her son take on the role of being king."

"I don't feel like she would, though, knowing that this was made for Reya."

"Ranvir, it's all about perspective. It's how you view this gift. You can look at it that way, or you can look at it as taking the next step and knowing your history of your kingdom to become the best king you can be."

"Yeah, I guess so."

"Happy birthday, Ranvir! You truly are a blessing."

Mangus left the room. Ranvir took a long look at the book. He put his fingers on the cover of the book. He was about to open it, but knowing that this book was never meant to be given to him, he decided not to. He discarded the book and hid it somewhere in his room where he couldn't find it. He never came across the book until now.

All the memories came rushing back through his head. Although he never bothered to look at it when he was thirteen years old, he ceased the opportunity to see what this book was all about now that there was a chance he could become king.

Chapter 5

Ranvir touched the front of the cover. There was a part of him that wanted to read it, but then the other part wanted to put the book back on the shelf where it should've stayed. He opened the book very slowly. His eyes were glued to each page. As he kept reading, that's when he came across the chapter about the fate-rose. He read the description carefully.

"This rose can tell you your fate before it even happens. Wanna know your fate, find one in a forest near you. Look into the rose and know your fate before it even happens. Seek help from the one and only enchantress, Elenor, for more details. Although with this rose there comes a . . ."

That was all that Ranvir read. Reading that there was a rose that could change his whole life around was all that he needed. He knew this could be his chance to see if Agatha would come back for him and if he would end up with a queen.

"This rose could be the answer to everything! This could change my entire life! I might become king after all."

Ranvir got so cocky that he failed to read about the consequences that come with it. There was also a map that came with finding Elenor. He took that with him in case he could not find the fate-rose.

He set off into the forest on his horse after his dad went to sleep for the night. It was the first time in years that he stepped outside the kingdom in years. He finally felt free for once. He knew he didn't have to act like a prince for the time he was out in the forest. When he arrived at the forest, he checked every flower but did not come across any roses.

"Come on! Where are they!" Ranvir shouted.

He knew that he was going to have to seek help from Elenor because he was having so much trouble finding it. Getting to Elenor's hut was a challenge. It was all a dark path to get there and out, but Ranvir was willing to do whatever it took to find the fate-rose.

After tripping, getting his clothes caught in twigs, and stepping on stones, he made it to Elenor's hut.

"Um, excuse me? Elenor? My name is Ranvir. I'm the prince of Monrock. I was looking to see if you could help me find something."

Elenor came out from the shadows. Most people expect an enchantress to be pretty and beautiful, but Elenor had a bit of a dark side to her. Her hair was so curly that people had often mistaken her for Medusa. She would always wear dark eyeshadow and black lipstick to help her stand out more.

Ranvir stood still as a statue not knowing that the person walking toward him was Elenor.

"Ranvir, the son of Mangus?" Elenor asked.

"Yes. Are you Elenor?" Ranvir asked.

"Yes, I am."

"Really? But I thought an enchantress was supposed to be—"

"Pretty? I know, I get that a lot. I don't wanna be like every enchantress, so I decided to add a little dark to my part. I thought it would be creative."

"Yeah, it's very creative. I never would've thought about it that way."

"So what's a young prince like you doing out here alone in the forest? Aren't you supposed to be getting ready to become king, son?"

"Well, about that. You see, I don't really want to become king."

"Why's that?"

"Well, after my mom and sister died, I saw the struggles my dad went through taking on the task of being king alone, and I know that is a life that I don't want. I just think by having a queen by my side will help with everything. I could've had that, but my girlfriend of six years left me a year ago and never came back. After that happened, I just don't know if I want to take on the task of being the king."

"I'm sorry to hear that, Ranvir. I heard about what happened to your mom and sister a long time ago. I couldn't imagine what that was like for you and your father. As far as the whole queen thing goes, I don't think you need one to be successful."

"Ugh! Not you too! Jeez, I'm getting tired of everyone saying that."

"Whoa. Relax, my child. You're here for a reason obviously. You didn't just come here to tell me your sad story. If I were to guess, you came to look for guidance or something. What can I help you with?"

"Well, my dad gave me this book of the legends of Monrock when I was thirteen years old, but I never read it until now. I came across the legend of the fate-rose."

Elenor's smile turned into a frown. Never in one hundred years has she ever had another case of the fate-rose. She was scared it was going to turn into another case.

"I read that it can tell one's fate before they even know. If I find the rose, it can tell me if Agatha will come back for me or if I'll end up with a queen by my side. I was wondering if you knew where I could find the fate-rose."

Elenor took a moment to answer. "Ranvir, I'm guessing you did not read about the consequences that come with his rose."

"Huh? What consequences?"

"I'll take that as a yes that you did not read that part. That's what they all say."

"That's what who says?"

"Ranvir, come. Walk with me. I need to show you something."

Elenor guided Ranvir up the stairs and into the room where her crystal ball was.

"What's this all about? What does this have to do with the fate-rose?"

"Ranvir, I must warn you. This rose is what you think it is. You clearly did not read about the consequences that come with this rose. So look carefully into my crystal ball and listen to everything I'm about to tell you."

She started to work her magic crystal ball. Ranvir looked closely into it and saw another prince with the same issue.

"The origin of the rose starts here. Before I became the most powerful enchantress of the forest, there was one before me. She made this rose for herself. She wanted to know where her life would be in ten years, so she made up a whole bunch of spells about fate and put them into a rose. The rose at first worked just fine. It gave her anything she wanted to see. However, when she died of old age, the rose started to lose its power and started to act crazy. The rose was nowhere to be found by the time she was deceased. We now go into the story of Prince Felix. His case comes from having an arranged marriage. He wouldn't know who he was marrying until he saw the girl walk down the aisle. Fearing that he would not love the girl he would be marrying, he took a moment to himself into the woods. He came across the rose. Without even knowing, he started to think out loud to himself.

"'If only there was a way to know who the girl I will be marrying will be,' he said.

"As soon as he spoke the words, the rose started to work its magic. The rose revealed who his wife would be. The prince was relieved to know the answer that he was seeking. His excitement soon turned into disaster. He immediately fell into a deep sleep. Once his family knew he was missing, they set out to find him. After three days of searching, they found him unconscious. When he finally woke up after a three-day sleep, he had no memory of what happened and went on with his normal routine. Three days later, he fell to the ground weak and could not get up no matter how hard he tried. His parents immediately came to see me as they were confused on what was going on. I myself had no idea what was wrong with him, as I had no history of the rose at the time. As the days went on, Prince Felix started to become weaker and weaker to the point where he could no longer walk. Eventually, his body gave out and he passed away. More cases started to happen, and I had no idea why it was happening. When one case finally mentioned a rose, that's when I connected the pieces of the puzzle together. It was the fate-rose that was causing this. I tried very hard to find a cure to it or even its magic, but I had no idea what the previous enchantress used, so there was nothing that I could do. When people started to drop like flies, that's when I took the action to banish the rose so nobody could find it, and no cases have happened again."

Ranvir couldn't believe what he saw. He had no idea why he overlooked what the book said.

"I haven't had a case in one hundred years, Ranvir. I don't want to start this process all over again."

"But it's been one hundred years. Who knows if the rose is still powerful?"

"Seriously? After seeing that vision and knowing what could happen to you, you still want me to tell you where to find the rose?"

"Well, I mean, it's worth the try, right?"

"I think your head is still spinning from watching the vision. You can't possibly want any contact with the rose after seeing that."

"But it's been one hundred years. What if the magic wore off?"

"Why take the chance, though, on the what-if? I'm sorry, Ranvir, but I can't tell you where the fate-rose is. I'm sorry, but I don't want another case of broken hearts again from the parents of those who fell as the victims. I can't go down that path again. I can't."

"But the rose is the only way to know if I'll be a successful king."

"Ranvir, I know in my heart that you'll be a great king. You don't need a rose to tell you that. You have to believe it for yourself for it to come true."

Ranvir was frustrated at the fact that he wasn't going to find out his fate. He wished that Elenor would understand where he was coming from.

"You seem like a nice kid. You look like you have it all together. Why risk your life for a rose? You will be all right leading on your own. Is there anything else that you needed?"

"No, but thanks."

"No problem. Don't forget, Ranvir, you're your own person. You'll be fine leading on your own if you have to. I know you have what it takes."

Ranvir rolled his eyes when Elenor wasn't looking. He felt like he was back to square one now.

"Is there anything I can get you before you see your way out?"

"Just some water will be fine."

"All right. Give me one second."

Elenor went to grab him some water. Ranvir secretly started to snoop around to see if he could find anything about the fate-rose. He looked in all her drawers and boxes and could not find anything. Before he gave up, he stubbed his toe on one of the bottom drawers. He looked into the drawer and saw a map that was labeled "rose" on it. He heard Elenor coming back up the stars and quickly shoved the map into his pocket. Despite Elenor's warning and the consequences that come with the rose, he didn't bother to listen and continued to be cocky, thinking that the rose was over one hundred years old and probably lost all its magic.

Elenor gave him his water, which he drank down quickly. Ranvir made his way to the door.

"All right, Ranvir. I hope you have a great night! Remember what I told you."

"Thanks."

Ranvir stepped out of her house. His grin started to show. He pulled out the map to where she banished the fate-rose. He went back to his horse and made his way to the location.

"Looks like I'm about to find out my fate!"

After another two hours of finding the forest where Elenor banished the rose, Ranvir finally made it to the location. He searched for about a good thirty minutes before finally coming across the rose. He had no words. He was about to find out his fate. He could feel more butterflies in his stomach.

Ranvir picked up the rose. He closed his eyes and took a deep breath. He was about to find out his future. He looked into the rose. He saw the rose work its magic.

"Ok, so it looks like I become king, but do I have a—"

The rose showed to have a girl beside him. It didn't show her face, as it was still processing his future.

"Oh my gosh! I'm going to have a queen. Looks like I won't have to fight with my dad anymore about it!"

The rose was about to reveal who it was. "This is it!"

Before the rose could reveal who it was, Ranvir started to feel sleepy. He brushed it off as he thought he was just tired from being out all night. He walked around to help him stay awake. As soon as the rose revealed who it was, Ranvir, all of a sudden, was knocked out cold and hit the side of his head as he fell. Ranvir was now in full effect of the rose. He was now in a deep sleep.

The sun started to rise. Mangus awoke and headed toward Ranvir's room. He didn't know which Ranvir he was going to get. He knocked on the door.

"Ranvir, rise up!" Mangus said.

Mangus was in complete shock to see Ranvir's room a mess and Ranvir not in his room.

"Ranvir? Ranvir! Ranvir, I don't know what game you're playing, but it's not funny."

Magus looked all around in the palace but could not find him. He looked outside but still didn't see Ranvir anywhere.

"Cecila, have you seen Ranvir anywhere?" Mangus asked.

"No, I haven't. Why?"

"I can't find him anywhere."

"I didn't see his horse in the stables. My guess is that he went outside the kingdom."

Mangus started to worry. He immediately ran to the stables to grab his horse.

"Soldiers! Search party! We need to find Ranvir!" Mangus shouted.

Mangus and his soldiers raced outside the kingdom to search for Ranvir. Mangus had his horse track down Ranvir's scent. He had a lot of thoughts running through his mind. He knew he needed to find Ranvir as quickly as possible.

Chapter 6

"Ranvir! Ranvir! Son, where are you?" Mangus shouted.

All day and all night, Mangus and his soldiers looked for Ranvir, but so far, they could not find him anywhere.

Dang. How far could this boy have gone? Mangus thought.

Mangus's heart was racing so fast. He had all these thoughts running through his mind. He knew he needed to find Ranvir and fast.

"Sir, we've gone far for the night. Do we stop for tonight?" one soldier asked.

"NO! We keep going until we find my son! You hear me! Do not stop looking!" Mangus shouted.

"Aye, sir," he said.

More hours passed, and they still had no luck in finding Ranvir. Mangus started to panic even more. He was worried that Ranvir was in serious danger.

"Sir! We found him!" one shouted.

Mangus made his horse make a beeline straight toward where his soldiers were standing. He was starting to fear for the worst. He thought something seriously happened to his son. By the time he made his way over there, he ran straight toward Ranvir and got on his knees. Seeing his son unconscious made his eyes all watery.

"Ranvir? Son, can you hear me?"

He held his head up to support it. He listened for a pulse and was relieved to hear one. He knew Ranvir was alive. Mangus noticed the bruise on the side of his head. He thought that's what made him unconscious.

"We need to get him help. This could be a serious injury. We don't have time to make it back into the kingdom in case it is severe."

"Right, my lord. Let's go!" one said.

Mangus and his soldiers rode all into the forest looking for help. He was worried his son had a serious condition, as he didn't see what happened. They rode through each forest and could not find help. They finally came across Elenor's hut. Mangus banged on the door.

"Please! Someone help! It's my son!" Mangus shouted.

Elenor slowly opened the door. She was shocked to see Ranvir unconscious. She feared he encountered the fate-rose.

"Ranvir?" Elenor asked.

"You know my son?" Mangus asked.

"Apparently, yes. He came by my hut not too long ago looking for the fate-rose."

"That's impossible! My son would never do something like that. I don't know what has gotten in his head."

"Well, I hate to say it, but I think he was trying to. Why else would he want to know if he was going to have a queen by his side or not?"

"But you banished that rose for good, right?"

"Yes. He shouldn't have been able to find it. Anyway, what happened to him?"

"I don't know. We found him like this. He probably hit his head while riding back. He must've fell off his horse."

Elenor checked out his bruise. The fate-rose was running through her mind, but she knew it was impossible for one to find the fate-rose without knowing where she banished it. She started to take proper care of his wound.

"He may have a slight concussion. Ride back slowly and let him rest for a day or two. He'll be all right."

"I really do appreciate it. Elenor, right?"

"Yes, sir."

"Thank you for the help. We'll be seeing our way out."

Mangus and his soldiers rode back into the kingdom. Elenor was concerned about the fate-rose. She decided to take another step forward, which was to banish the rose to another place so it would be more impossible to find. She went into her drawers to look for her map. The map was not

"Good. The kingdom was definitely not the same without you. Glad to see you up."

Ranvir smiled. "I appreciate it."

"Of course. You deserve the best."

Just then, everyone started to race toward something. People started to whisper and talk.

"Hey, what's going on?" Ranvir asked.

"I have no idea. Only one way to find out, though," Mangus said.

They started to follow the crowd. They both had no idea what was going on. Everyone could not believe their eyes at what they were seeing. By the time both Ranvir and Mangus made it to the gate where everyone was going, Ranvir could not believe his eyes. His mouth dropped to the ground. His hands started to shake. He couldn't get any words out of his mouth. Was he seeing what he thought he was seeing? He pinched himself to make sure he was seeing what everyone else was.

"Is that really her?" people whispered.

"A-Agatha?" Ranvir said.

There stood Agatha, Ranvir's girlfriend who left him for a year without an explanation. She stood there by her horse with her hair flowing in the wind. She had a guilty look on her face. Ranvir started to feel teary. He could not get any words out. He didn't know if he should be happy or upset to see Agatha.

Chapter 7

Ranvir's heart started pounding. It grew louder and louder. He couldn't believe that Agatha came back. After all this time, he thought she was gone for good, but there she was standing right before his eyes. All these thoughts were running through his head: Where was she all this time? Why did she not come back? Did she still love him? Tears started to build up in his eye sockets.

"Ranvir," Agatha said.

Ranvir's heart started beating louder and louder. It was so loud, he could hear it in his ears. Ranvir couldn't move. He wanted to run toward her, but he was stuck.

"Ranvir, I know, I know you're probably upset with me, but, please, just hear me out. Please. Just for a moment," Agatha said.

Ranvir looked at everyone, giving them the hint that he wanted to speak with her alone. Mangus gathered everyone away from both of them.

"Whatever you have to say to him, you can say it in front of me too!" Cecila said.

"It's OK, Cecila. I can handle it," Ranvir said.

"Are you sure?"

"Yes, I'll be OK."

"All right. Let me know if you need me."

"I will."

Cecila walked away with the rest of the crowd. She thought Agatha had some nerve to come back after a year with no explanation. As much as she wanted to support Ranvir and defend him, she respected his wishes.

Ranvir started to walk toward Agatha. Agatha was very nervous on how Ranvir was going to react to her leaving him behind for a year. Ranvir stood right in front of her. He did not say one word, only a gesture to her to allow her to explain herself.

"I know what you're thinking, Ranvir. Why didn't I come back like I promised? Why did I not bother to write? I just, I just . . . I don't know. I just needed space. After everything that has happened, I just felt like I needed to clear my head for a while. Everything was just so overwhelming for me. I thought by being away would help me cope with my emotions, but I-I don't know."

Ranvir continued to just stand there. He did not speak one word to her. Not one. Agatha waited for him to say something, but Ranvir did not say anything.

"I know you're probably very mad and upset with me, and that's all right. You have every right to be. I made the biggest mistake of my life. I was the one who abandoned you. I was selfish. I didn't bother to think about your feelings and how it must have made you feel. That was wrong of me to do so. I just wish you could stop staring at me and remaining quiet. Don't do this to me, Ranvir. Can you just talk to me? Please. Just say one sentence, a word, a sound, something!"

Ranvir placed both of his hands on her cheeks. Agatha was at a loss for words on what Ranvir was about to say. He could either be happy or very mad that she came back for him. Ranvir struggled to get words out of his mouth. Ranvir could feel his tears started to form and make their way down his cheeks.

"Why were you gone for so long, Agatha? Why?" Ranvir squeaked.

Agatha also felt tears coming on herself. She felt so bad for what she did to Ranvir that she could not contain her emotions.

"I'm sorry, Ranvir."

She hugged him. Ranvir was shocked at first but slowly eased his way into it. He hugged her tighter. The girl whom he was with for six years was now back in his life, but he didn't know what it meant for them. They pulled back, and Ranvir wiped away his tears and tried to get himself together.

"Agatha, take a walk with me. We need to talk about this. Let's take a walk through the garden like we always did."

"I'd like that."

They started to take a walk to clear the air. Cecila kept her eye on Agatha. She thought it was very weird that she came out of the blue after a year.

"Remember this place? I used to sneak out of the castle every night to meet up with you," Ranvir said.

"Of course, I do. How could I forget?" Agatha said.

"Well, you seemed to have forgotten me," Ranvir said painfully.

Agatha looked at Ranvir. She knew deep inside that he was hurting. She felt so bad that she was the reason behind why he was hurting in the first place.

"Ranvir, I-I feel so bad for what I did."

"Do you care to explain?"

"Yes. You deserve to hear the explanation that I never gave to you. After being overwhelmed with taking care of my brothers and my life changing, I just felt lost. I felt like I was becoming a different person. I wasn't sure who I truly was anymore. That's when I made the drastic decision to leave the kingdom for a while. I know I promised that I would come back for you after a month, but I didn't. Why? I had the choice. I could either come back to you and continue my life in the kingdom or not come back and continue to be stress-free and allowed to live my life and be free. When it came to making the decision, I honestly felt like that you would've been better off without me. I felt like I was being a burden to you with you being the prince. But, clearly, I was wrong, seeing how hurt you are."

"So why did you come back? What made you after a year?"

"Well, the truth is that I never forgot you. I literally thought about you every day. My heart hurt not being beside you, but for once, I felt free focusing on myself without making others happy. One day, you just were on my mind a lot, and I couldn't stop thinking about you. I was hesitant whether I should return. My biggest fear was that you would want nothing to do with me after what I did. Although I thought the worst, I knew that it was better to try and hope for a good reaction than not try at all. That's why I came back because I missed you."

Ranvir was overcome with emotion. His tears became visible again. He did his best to get himself together.

"You have every right to be mad and upset with me. Do you have anything you want to say? If you want to shout and scream at me, I deserve it."

"Agatha, I just . . . I'm just so hurt from what you did to me. Like you don't understand. I was hurt for a long time. You were my first love. I literally thought you were the only one for me. You made me feel loved. I loved you. With everything that I had. I was actually going to propose to you the day you left me. You decided to leave me for a month, which turned into a year, for what? Just to have some independence? You don't think that I wish for independence and to be free? I don't, Agatha. I have my duties. I never once considered you a burden. If anything, you were my everything. I felt like I could talk to you about anything, and you made my day better. After what you did, it felt like a punch in the gut. You were so selfish to do this to me. You will never understand how hurt I was when you left. You will never understand unless the tables were turned. I still have the ring in my drawer. Do you understand how bad it hurt me still seeing it thinking about that horrible day, which could've been the best day in my life? I just . . . I'm so hurt. You have no idea. I thought you would be my queen. Instead, you left me alone in the wings waiting for you to return, but you never came. You didn't even bother to write to me to tell me what was going on. You could have easily done so, but you didn't. You ghosted me. I didn't want to believe that it was over, but I eventually had to come to the conclusion that it might've been. I'm very confused, Agatha. I don't know where we even stand now. I don't know."

Agatha started to cry. To hear that Ranvir was going to propose to her and how hurt he was from what she did to him made her feel like a monster. Her tears started to become impossible to hide.

"Ranvir, I am so sorry. I know that you don't want to hear my excuses, but to hear what I did to you makes me feel even more horrible. You have every right not wanting anything to do with me anymore. I deserve that. I was no girlfriend to you after what I did. Just know that I never stopped loving you for the time I was gone. I am so sorry for hurting you and making you feel unworthy. If you want me to go, I will. You have every right to hate me after what I did."

When Ranvir heard Agatha pour her heart out, he knew that she truly was sorry. Although he was still hurting from what she did to him, Ranvir knew in his heart that he would never hate her. He turned toward her and held her hand.

"Am I upset that you left me? Yes. Am I hurt by what you did? Yes. Am I angry at you for not even bothering to write? Yes. But to hate you?

That's a very strong word. Yes, I am upset, hurt, and angry, but I could never hate you, Agatha."

Agatha smiled knowing that Ranvir doesn't hate her. Her worst fear was behind her. She was hoping that Ranvir would give her another chance.

"All this time of being away, I truly am sorry, Ranvir, with all my heart. Do you think that maybe we could start over? Maybe even give me another chance? I will support your decision whatever you choose. You have every right not to take me back."

Ranvir sighed. He didn't know what to say. A part of him was still hurt and did not want to take Agatha back, but another part of him missed her and wanted her back. He thought about it for a few seconds.

"Agatha, I love you. You know that, right?"

"Of course!"

"I mean, I was going to propose to you. That's how much I loved you. My love for you hasn't changed when you left. It probably never will. Although I am still very hurt by what you did, there is always a good side to me. Despite all the hurt, I am willing to give you another chance. It's probably going to take a while for our relationship to get back to the way it was. We just need to take it one day at a time. But, yes, I forgive you and will take you back."

Agatha smiled really hard. She did not expect for Ranvir to take her back, so this was such a huge weight lifted off her shoulders. They hugged each other tight with tears running down their cheeks.

"I love you so much, Ranvir! I promise I will never hurt or leave you again. I already made that mistake, and I intend not to do it again."

"I love you too! I know you won't. I just missed you so much."

"I did too, Ranvir."

Ranvir didn't hesitate at all to kiss her. Agatha slowly eased her way into it, not holding back at all. This moment was perfect for both of them. No hurt, no sadness. They forgot for a moment that they were in the kingdom. Ranvir never wanted to let her go. He could've stayed like that forever, but, eventually, they would have to come back to reality. They pulled away slowly, and Agatha rested her head on his shoulder before holding his hand. They watched the sunset together for the first time in a year. Ranvir was so happy that Agatha was back in his life again.

Chapter 8

"I'm coming, Ranvir! I'm coming!" Elenor said.

Elenor was halfway to the kingdom. She tried her very best to get there as fast as she could. She knew if she didn't get there sooner, Ranvir would be a goner before she could even warn Mangus.

"Please, Ranvir, stay alive! I can't deal with another case," Elenor said.

Three days passed, and everyone in the kingdom knew about Ranvir and Agatha getting back together. Mangus was very happy to see his son smiling again. Agatha took the time to see her family and friends again. Ranvir and Agatha also spent those three days for themselves to catch up on how much they missed over a year.

"So did you like being on your own for a while?" Ranvir asked.

"It was amazing, but at the same time, I did miss having someone to talk to. It was hard sometimes, but I managed to get through it," Agatha said.

"I'm really happy you're back, Agatha. Life just wasn't the greatest without you. I know that's corny to say but—"

"It's fine, Ranvir. That's so you. I wouldn't have it any other way."

"That's a relief to hear."

"So tell me. What's been happening in the kingdom?" Agatha asked.

"A lot actually. It's been a real battle," Ranvir said.

"Really? Why?"

"Well, my dad wants me to become king early. I just don't feel like I'm ready to become king. I don't know if I'll be."

"Why?"

"I saw the struggle my dad had when he had to rule the kingdom. I'm not so sure if I want to follow . . ."

Ranvir paused for a moment. He just realized that he had Agatha back. He thought he could finally have the courage to become king by having Agatha as his queen.

"Listen. You're coming to the ball tonight, right?"

"Well, yeah! I wouldn't miss it for the world. That is where we met after all."

"Great! I'll see you there tonight!"

"Is everything OK?"

"Oh, yeah, just fine! I'll see you later."

Ranvir ran back to the castle. He thought now was his chance to propose to Agatha, a moment he thought he would never get back. He started to dig around the room to find the ring. Because of him having a rage a week ago, he threw the ring somewhere and now was struggling to find it. There was a knock on his door.

"Who is it?" Ranvir asked.

"Cecila," Cecila said.

"Come in."

Cecila walked in the room to find Ranvir looking for something.

"What's going on, Ranvir?"

"Looking for something."

"What might that be?"

Ranvir hit his head under his bed. He started to get frustrated that he could not find the ring.

"I'm looking for the ring for Agatha."

"The ring? As in the proposal ring that you were planning to propose to her with before she took off and left you?"

"Well, if you put it that way, yes. Can you please help me find it?"

Cecila started to help him look around for the ring. They both had no luck finding it until Cecila finally found it under his legends book.

"Found it."

"For real? Oh, thank goodness! You're a lifesaver."

"Can I ask what you need it for?"

"What do you think?"

"Are you saying that you're actually going to propose to her?"

"Yes, tonight."

"Tonight? She's only been back for three days and you want to propose to her?"

"I know, but I wanted to start on what I never got to do. What better way to propose to her in the place where we first met?"

"But, Ranvir, she left you for a year. She could have changed. How do you know that she's the girl you want to be with for the rest of your life?"

"I just know, Cecila."

"But I watched you get hurt, Ranvir. I don't want you to again."

"I won't. She opened up to me and poured her heart on how sorry she was. I just know she's the one for me."

"Is she, though, Ranvir?"

"Why don't you want her to be my queen?"

"It's not that I don't, Ranvir. I just think it's weird that she was gone for a year, and out of the blue, she just decides to come back. I find that very odd. Like, why now?"

"I asked her about that. She really missed me. She did for all the time she was gone."

"Well, if I'm being honest, if she really missed you, she would've come back after a month like she promised."

"I know, but we all make mistakes."

"Ranvir, I just feel like you want to propose to her so you can become king like your father wants and that you have the queen you need."

"Well, all of that is not true. I love Agatha with everything that I have. I wanted her to be my queen a year ago."

"And what happened?"

"I just don't know why you just can't be happy for me. It seems like you're trying to talk me out of proposing."

Cecila was shocked hearing Ranvir say that. As his friend, she did not want to see him get hurt again. She was only looking out for him knowing that he's been down that path before.

"Ranvir, it's not that I'm not happy for you. I just don't want to see you get hurt again. I was there when she left you. It hurt me to see you upset. I'm just worried you're jumping into an engagement because you feel like you have to. An engagement should be a time of happiness of where you want to be."

"I am happy, Cecila. I want to marry Agatha, not just to make her queen but because I love her. I wouldn't have tried to do so in the first place if I didn't love her."

"But why do you feel like you have to rush into it now? Wouldn't you rather wait to make sure she came back for the right reason?"

"She did come back for the right reason, I can reassure you."

"I believe you, Ranvir. I just hope I can believe Agatha. I just ask that you think wisely before jumping into something like this. I will support you no matter what choice you make. I'll see you at the ball tonight."

Cecila left the room. Ranvir was confused why Cecila was questioning his decision to propose when she was on his side a year ago. He brushed it off and started to get ready for the ball.

"Ranvir? You ready?" Mangus asked.

"Almost, Dad."

Mangus came into the room. He was happy to see his son smiling and upbeat again. He thought that Ranvir would soon regain the confidence to become king.

"Don't you look handsome."

"Only for the best."

"I'm glad she came back. I haven't seen you this happy since the last time she was here."

"This is going to be the best night of life part two."

"Part two?"

Ranvir pulled the ring out from his pocket. Mangus was surprised to see that Ranvir was going to try and propose to Agatha this time.

"You don't think she's going to run away this time, do you?"

"No, of course not! I would hate to have déjà vu."

"I'm happy for you, son. It takes a strong person to forgive someone like that."

"It wasn't easy, but I know that Agatha is the only one for me."

"Don't get too cocky now, son. I thought the same thing when I was eighteen. Yes, your mother and I were friends all our lives, but we didn't start dating until I turned nineteen. I was with a girl before your mother, but, sadly, she found someone better, and so did I—your mother. You may say that, but just know that won't always be the case."

"I can't imagine my life with anyone else but her."

"I'm glad you found your happily ever after. Keep getting ready. The ball is starting soon."

"I'll be there."

Mangus left the room. Ranvir continued to get ready. He looked at the ring one more time. He held it close.

"Please let it go right this time. Let her say yes."

Ranvir made his way to the ballroom. He waited for Agatha. When she arrived, Ranvir was stunned. She looked so beautiful.

"Looking great tonight, m' lady!" Ranvir said.

"Thank you!"

"Are you excited?"

"Very! I've missed these dances. That is how we fell in love after all."

"And now we can fall in love all over again."

Agatha smiled and held his arm as they both walked to the ballroom together. Ranvir's nerves were starting to kick in. He could already feel his hands shaking. The ball started, and both Ranvir and Agatha were having the time of their lives. They couldn't remember the last time they danced together. As the ball was halfway over, Ranvir ceased the opportunity for the perfect moment to propose.

"Hello, my people. How are we tonight?" Mangus said.

Everyone cheered.

"Glad to hear! I want to take this time to welcome Agatha back into the kingdom. We all missed you. We're glad to have you back," Mangus said.

Agatha smiled as everyone clapped.

"I'm going to take this time to hand this over to my Ranvir, soon to be the new king."

Everyone clapped.

"Thank you all for coming out tonight. We love holding our annual balls. They mean a lot not only to our kingdom but also, most importantly, to me. I don't mean to single anyone out, but seven years ago, I met a wonderful young lady here in the ballroom. We were together for six years until our relationship went on hiatus for a year. Three days ago, she came back into my life. I have never been happier in my life. She has made me a better person. Agatha, you have changed my life for the better. You were my first love. You are the only one for me. I don't know where I could be if I never met you here on the dance floor. Before you left, there was something I wanted to do but never got the chance to, and I will not live another day if I never got the opportunity to ask you."

Ranvir got down on one knee and pulled out the ring. Agatha covered her mouth in shock. She started to feel teary. Everyone started to get excited.

"Agatha, you are the only one for me. I want you to be my queen. I knew that for a long time. Will you marry me?"

Agatha's tears became uncontrollable. She couldn't get any words out. She was not expecting Ranvir to propose to her after what she did to him.

"Yes! Yes!" Agatha said in excitement.

Everyone started to cheer. Ranvir smiled and placed the ring on her finger. He stood up and kissed her passionately. Everyone was happy for the couple. Cecila smiled, but she was still unsure of Ranvir's decision of marrying Agatha.

"I love you!" Agatha.

"I love you too!" Ranvir said.

A slow dance came on, and Ranvir and Agatha shared one together officially as an engaged couple—the future king and queen.

Elenor still was nowhere near the kingdom. She never pictured that it would be hard to get there from the forest. She already started to fear for the worst. She hoped to get there in time before Ranvir became weak.

Chapter 9

Two days after Ranvir proposed to Agatha, the kingdom was throwing an engagement party for the couple; most importantly, they soon would be the new king and queen of Monrock. Ranvir started to get ready. He never thought this day would come. Soon, Agatha would be his queen, and he would no longer have the stress of running a kingdom by himself. There was a knock on his door.

"Come in," Ranvir said.

Mangus walked in with some outfits. He was beaming with joy knowing that his son was finally going to take his place.

"I brought some outfits that you might want to wear tonight and your coronation. These are the outfits that were passed down from your grandfather, to me, and now to you."

Ranvir looked at each outfit. He started to try them on one by one. Mangus had no words to describe how handsome his son looked.

"You look just like me when I was your age."

"Is that a good thing?"

"Of course, it is. I remember being so nervous about my coronation. I remember not even wanting to go out there."

"What made you do so?"

"I just knew my place. I needed to do what was right for my people and the kingdom."

"Also, how did you know Mom was the one for you?"

"Well, after I went through that heartbreak, I realized she was there for me as a friend from the beginning. I never knew that we could be anything more than friends, but I gave it a chance, and then we became engaged and soon married. She gave me the best years of life. One thing I will say, Ranvir, is to not take anything for granted. Life could change in an instant. That's when I lost the two most important people in my life."

"I wish Mom and Reya could be here for my special day. They would've loved to see me get married."

"Me too. I know for sure that they will be watching it from the sky."

"Dad, do you sometimes wish that you could turn back time and stop their deaths from happening?"

"Well, I'm not sure, Ranvir. As much as I would say yes, I wouldn't. Yes, I still grieve them every day, but life goes on. Everything happens for a reason. You were made to be the heir. I wish it could've happened in a way that wasn't so sad, but it happened. Nothing more we can do. The most important thing I would never change is being your father. I may have lost your mother and sister, but I still had you. You made me the person I was made to be. You were my motivation to try harder."

Ranvir started to cry. He never heard his father say something like this before. He hugged him. Mangus stroked his hair.

"Thanks, Dad."

"Always, son. I know you and I got off to a rocky start about making your coming of age early, but I wanted to ask, how are you feeling about it now?"

"I mean, I still have mixed emotions about it. I have Agatha, though, so I feel like I'm ready."

"Son, I know you had your hesitation going into this, but I don't want you to put all your roses in one basket. Agatha is a wonderful girl, and I am happy that you are finally getting the queen you want, but you need to ask yourself something. What is your purpose? Why do you truly want to become king? You always have to have a purpose for what you do in life. Is your purpose because of Agatha?"

"No."

"The only reason I ask is because you had no intention of being king until you had a queen. Why do you feel the reason you need a queen to make you successful?"

"Dad, please, I really don't wanna rehash this conversation again, OK? Let's just focus on tonight and celebrate the engagement."

"You're right. My last question is, are we having your coronation before the wedding?"

"Yeah, I guess so. It only makes sense to."

"Good. I'm glad. Well, I guess I'll see you down there tonight, the future king of Monrock."

"Yes, you will."

"See you soon, son."

Ranvir continued to get ready. Cecila made her way to Ranvir's room to apologize for having doubts about yesterday and to share how happy she is for him, but her conversation became a different story after overhearing something she wished she never did. As she walked through the castle, she walked by the room where Agatha was getting ready. She heard her talk about Ranvir. She didn't want to eavesdrop, but she was willing to protect her best friend at all costs. She heard the conversation go on between Agatha and one of her friends named Ameila.

"So are you excited about marrying the love of your life?" Ameila asked.

"Yeah, I guess so," Agatha said.

"You guess? What kind of response is that?"

"Ameila, you know the whole reason behind it all."

"Agatha, I thought you changed. Are you still up to your old ways?"

"Ameila, you know that I never truly loved Ranvir. I mean, don't get me wrong, I do love him, but the only reason I'm with him is to become the queen."

Cecila was in shock. She could not believe the words that came out of Agatha's mouth. Cecila tried so hard to bite her tongue with everything that she had.

"Agatha, that's not right. I don't know why you came back in the first place if you were just up to your old trick again. I think you made the right decision to leave him for a year so you wouldn't hurt him, but now to hear that you're doing this! That's going to break him even more. Why do that to him?"

"Well, word on the street was that I heard he was probably going to become king early and that he didn't want to become king without a queen, so what better way to come back and step into the role? That is what he wanted after all—a queen."

"But he loves you, Agatha. What if he finds out the truth?"

"I never said I didn't love him. Not truly is what I said. He won't find out. I can assure you that. If he could fall for my story and my emotions about me coming back, there is no need to worry. Ranvir falls for almost everything. I feel bad that he's so vulnerable."

"I just hope you're right about this, Agatha. I would hate for this to come back to haunt you."

"It will be fine, Ameila. Everyone is going to get their wish."

"I hope so, Agatha."

Cecila was at a loss for words. Her suspicions about Agatha were right. She couldn't believe that Agatha was doing that to her best friend. She raced down the hall to warn Ranvir about Agatha's intentions. She knocked on the door several times.

"All right, I'm coming," Ranvir said. He opened the door. "Cecila? Hey, what brings you here? I didn't think I would see you today."

"Ranvir, I originally came here to apologize for having doubts yesterday and to say that I'm happy for you."

"I appreciate that. Originally? What made you change your mind?"

"Ranvir, I really hate to tell you this, but I would rather you find out from me than hear it from someone else. I overheard Agatha talking to her friend Ameila. She . . . Ugh. This is so hard to tell you. My gut was right. Agatha is not here for the right reason. I overheard her say that she's only using you for the throne."

Ranvir's heart started to pound. Hearing this news was a huge punch in the gut for him, although he thought that Cecila was only telling him that so he could call off the engagement.

"Ranvir, I'm really sorry that I had to tell you this, but I heard her say it loud and clear. I think you need to call off the engagement."

"I don't believe you."

Cecila was blindsided by his response. She never expected a response from Ranvir that was so negative.

"What?"

"I don't believe you, Cecila."

"Ranvir, why would I come all the way to your room to tell you something like this? I knew something was up the moment she came back. I gave her the benefit of the doubt but found out my thoughts about her were correct."

"I feel like you're just saying this to me because you don't want me to marry her."

"Are you kidding me! I have been nothing but supportive to you two from the beginning! Don't you dare sit there and say that to me when I have been your biggest supporter."

"Supportive? I don't think that's the word. Those three days that she has been back, I feel like you were acting nice to be nice. I didn't feel any support from you. If anything, I felt like you were never happy for me."

"Wow, Ranvir. Just keep saying that. That's not true. I supported you because you're my best friend! I was there for you when she hurt you and left you. I had every right to have my doubts about her, and look at what happened. I was right! I know this isn't news you want to hear, but if I wasn't such a good friend and cared about you, I wouldn't be telling you this. Did I want to tell you? No. But I didn't want to see you get hurt again, so that's why I'm telling you this now. The best thing to do right now is to call it all off. I know this is a hard thing to do, but I will be there for you no matter what."

"Or is this a coincidence that the engagement party is tonight and that I am getting married soon? If I'm being honest, Cecila, I feel like you're just jealous. I don't think you're happy for me. I don't think you have been since Agatha came into my life. I'm not calling off the engagement! Stop being jealous of her."

Cecila was livid at that point. She could not believe that Ranvir said she was jealous and thought she was making the whole thing up. She knew Ranvir had changed, and she didn't like that.

"Jealous! You think I'm jealous! You wish, Ranvir! You know what, you are not the same Ranvir that I've known my entire life. You have changed, and you know it! You are becoming a different Ranvir, and I don't like it! Agatha has taken you under her skin, and you refuse to come to your senses because you just want to believe that I would make something up like this! What happened to the Ranvir I first met? I'm done, Ranvir. You can find yourself a new best friend! And I'm not going to your engagement party tonight because, apparently, I'm jealous of Agatha! Good luck on your marriage! When she tells you the truth or when you find out from someone else, I don't wanna hear it! Have a great life!"

Cecila stormed out of the room and slammed the door. That was a lot for Ranvir to take in, but he needed to put that aside and be there for Agatha for the engagement party. By the time the party rolled around, Ranvir felt ready. As he was walking down the hall to meet up with Agatha, he felt a sharp pain in his side. He was confused why his side was hurting. As much as he thought, he figured he was just nervous and was just getting a cramp from the nerves. He brushed it aside and continued to walk. When he saw Agatha, he could not speak. She was so beautiful!

"You're so beautiful!" Ranvir whispered in her ear and kissed her cheek.

"You look handsome," Agatha said.

"Shall we?" Ranvir said.

"I'm ready," Agatha said.

They held each other's hands and walked toward the ballroom. Ranvir felt another sharp pain in his side. He shrieked in pain.

"Are you all right?" Agatha asked.

"Yeah, I think I just didn't drink enough water. I'll be all right."

"OK, if you say so."

They continued to make their way to the ballroom. Everyone started to cheer with excitement.

"Ladies and gentlemen, the future king and queen of Monrock!" Mangus shouted.

Everyone cheered louder. Ranvir and Agatha smiled. Ranvir looked over to see Cecila absent from the party. As much as he was upset from what had happened and that he and Cecila may have had a falling out, he focused his attention toward Agatha. Throughout the night, the party was a success until Ranvir started to feel light-headed.

"Are you all right, Ranvir? You look pale," Mangus asked.

"Yeah. I think it was just from all the dancing," Ranvir said.

Ranvir tried to stay focused, but he just was not feeling good. He suddenly felt dizzy and was trying to keep a clear focus, but the whole room was spinning around him. The pain in his sides grew worse.

"Ranvir, are you sure you're OK?" Agatha asked.

"Yes, I'm all right," Ranvir said.

"You look really flushed. Are you sure?"

"I think it's just hot in here. I probably just need some fresh air."

Ranvir took another step, and he fell to the floor. Pain was shooting up his body, and he was so dizzy. He started to feel weak.

"Ranvir!" Agatha shouted.

"Ranvir! Son! Can you hear me? Speak to me!" Mangus shouted.

Ranvir moaned in pain and could not get any words. Everyone started to crowd around him. Nobody knew what was going on. Mangus and Agatha helped Ranvir up and got him out of the room. As Mangus carried Ranvir outside the ballroom, Cecila saw and started to worry.

"Agatha, we need to get him to Elenor, the enchantress. We need to find out what's going on."

Mangus and Agatha ran toward the gate of the kingdom surprisingly to come face-to-face with Elenor.

"Elenor! Thank goodness you're here! It's Ranvir. We don't know what happened," Mangus stuttered.

Elenor took one good look at Ranvir. She knew that Ranvir was headed down a dark road at this moment.

"Mangus, since the moment you left my hut, I've been trying to tell you, Ranvir is in great danger."

Chapter 10

"Danger? What do you mean in danger?" Mangus asked.

Elenor could not find a way to tell Mangus that Ranvir encountered the fate-rose and that death would knock on his door in a nice way. She thought about how she was going to address the issue without making it too blunt.

"Mangus, there is no way to sugarcoat this, but Ranvir encountered the fate-rose. He's starting to experience the symptoms," Elenor said.

"What! But you said he was just suffering from a concussion. He even said that he did not encounter that rose!" Mangus said.

"That was before I found out he took my map to find where I banished it. Memory loss of the rose is the first sign the victim goes through after waking from the three-day slumber. I'm telling you, Mangus, Ranvir came to my hut that night and was looking to find it. He must have snuck into my drawers and took the map and found it. I'm sorry, Mangus, but your son has now become the first victim of the fate-rose in one hundred years."

"Ranvir! What were you thinking!" Mangus said.

"I'm so sorry, Dad," Ranvir said weakly.

Mangus was in disbelief. He could not believe he was now faced with the fact that he could lose Ranvir.

"But there's a cure, right?" Agatha asked.

"I'm afraid not. I'm sorry. I tried to find many cures for it, but nothing has worked. I don't know what the enchantress before me used in it, so I could try over a thousand things, but I don't know if anything will work."

"So what! I'm just supposed to accept the fact that my son is probably going to die!"

"Well, let's not get ahead of ourselves. I can do everything that I can to find a cure and maybe lessen the pain of the symptoms, but all you can do, Mangus, is to try and keep him alive longer."

"What do you mean longer?" Mangus asked.

"You see, Mangus, the power of the rose will only grow stronger to get to its weak victim. The victim falls into a three-day sleep, which was the first thing we both saw from what we thought was a concussion. He or she will then awaken and have no memory of the rose until he or she starts to experience the pain."

"Which already happened." Mangus said.

"Correct. The victim will soon start to become weaker the more energy he or she uses."

"Which explains why he was experiencing side pains and collapsed on the floor," Agatha said.

"Correct. The more energy the victim uses in his or her body, the weaker the victim will become. Soon enough, no more energy will be left, and then his or her body will fade away into the air."

Mangus started to fear for the worst. He had all the thoughts of losing Ranvir into his mind. He tried to remain positive, but how could he? His son could fall over and die any second simply by just walking.

"I'm so sorry. I really wish there was something more that I could do, but to help him stay alive longer, have him drink this potion every morning and night. It will help save his energy and take away some of the pains he is having. I will do my best to try and whip up a cure, but I would not get your hopes up."

"So does this mean the wedding is off?" Agatha asked.

"Agatha, the wedding should be a secondary concern right now," Elenor said.

"But what if something happens and I don't get to marry the love of my life? I couldn't live another day knowing that I would never get to marry the person I loved all my life," Agatha said.

Ranvir did his best to smile, but the pain was getting worse. He started to groan louder. Elenor gave him a spoonful of the potion to ease the pain.

"Please, Elenor," Ranvir said weakly.

"I just worry that his energy will drain. I would wait to see what happens first. If I don't find a cure within the next two days and he seems to be doing OK without growing weaker, go ahead. But I do not advise an actual wedding, though. If you have to marry him from his potential deathbed, so be it. It's better to be safe than sorry."

"Deal," Agatha said.

"Here's the potion, Mangus. Please do everything you can to keep Ranvir alive," Elenor said.

"I will. I will put him on bed rest. He won't get in or out unless he really needs to. I will not let anyone in to see him unless they really need to, and for a short period. Please, Elenor, do everything you can to try and find a cure."

"I will, Mangus! I don't want to deal with another death again. I'll try to do everything that I can."

Mangus carried Ranvir back to the castle. He placed him into bed and remained by his side for a while. Mangus explained to the kingdom everything that was happening to Ranvir, and he ordered everyone to stay outside of the castle until further notice for the sake of Ranvir. He would only allow a few small conversations if people wanted to see Ranvir. He also explained that Ranvir and Agatha might marry from the bedroom and that everyone could listen to the whole thing from the window if they wanted to be a part of it.

For an entire day, Ranvir lay in bed. He did not get up, nor did he speak to anyone. His pains were getting worse by the hour. He did not feel like a normal person to be stuck in bed away from the people he loved, but he knew he had to stay alive. Mangus came into his room.

"Time to take the potion, son," Mangus said.

The potion itself did not have a pleasant taste, but Ranvir had to put a brave face on and drink it as fast as he could. He groaned on how awful it tasted.

"I know. I know you hate it, but it will help with the pain."

"Why was I so stupid? Why did I have to find that rose? I knew I should've just listened to Elenor in the first place."

"Why did you feel a desire to seek it in the first place?"

"I-I was trying to find out if I would end up with a queen or not."

As much as Mangus wanted to be disappointed in Ranvir, he knew that he needed to just be there for his son knowing there was a possibility he could lose Ranvir.

"And did it tell you?"

"It was about to, but next thing I knew was that I was on the ground, and then I awoke in my bedroom. I had this dream, though. I was in a dark place. It was like I was stuck at the bottom and trying to work my way back up. When I did, I saw Mom and Reya. I thought I was dead. I thought my time was up, but all I can remember is them saying that I had a lot to give and that the kingdom needed me. As soon as they said that, I woke up."

"Really? Did they look any different?"

"Kinda. They both looked older but still the same."

"It's good that they both told you something encouraging."

"Definitely."

"All right, son. I'll let you get some rest. I'll be back to check on you a little later. You have your emergency bell. Just ring it if you need anything."

"I will. Thanks, Dad."

"I'll leave the window open so you can feel some fresh air and hear some civilization."

Mangus opened the window and walked out the room. Ranvir looked up at the ceiling for a long time before falling asleep. After being asleep for two hours, he was woken up by a conversation going on outside his window. He tried to block it out, but he couldn't. He slowly got out of bed and made his way to shut the window, but he heard Agatha's voice. He listened to the conversation.

"Agatha, you need to tell him!" Ameila said.

"But it's just going to make him weaker, and I'll be blamed for his death if I do," Agatha said.

"But being up to your old tricks again is . . . ? You need to do the right thing."

"Ameila, you knew all this time that I was only using Ranvir for the throne. I didn't see you try and stop me then."

"I was young at the time but soon knew it was wrong. That's why I told you that you should break up with him, but, instead, you left him for a year and came back with the same mind-set. I thought you would've changed your ways, Agatha, but you are still the same person with the same intentions."

"My way has always been to be the queen of Monrock! It will always be as long as Ranvir is alive. I just need Ranvir to stay alive, so we can get married and I'll become queen. If he passes, I'll still be the queen. I win either way. I will get that throne even if it means the end of Ranvir."

"I don't agree with this, Agatha. I think you just need to own up to your actions. The people of Monrock will disown you once they find out the truth."

"And they won't! We talked about this! I will be the queen!"

"How can you look at yourself in the mirror? Ranvir has put his heart and soul into you and has hurt for you, and the fact you are using him is very shallow."

"Think what you want. You don't have to be my maid of honor if you don't agree with me. I don't need you to become queen. I just need to marry Ranvir."

"I don't intend to be. I should frame you for this!"

"And you don't wanna do that. Unless you want to be banished as soon as I become queen. Nobody will believe you, so it'll be my word against yours! So do you really want to do that now?"

Ameila did not agree at all with what Agatha was doing, but she knew that nobody would believe her and didn't want to risk getting banished.

"I just wish you would do the right thing, Agatha."

"Oh, I am. I am becoming the queen. Ranvir will never find out! He's just rotting away in his bed as we speak. Now, if you excuse me, I must go write my vow to someone whom I don't truly love. I need to make sure it's not too emotional so it can save his energy. I need him to make it to the 'I do' part, and the rest will be history. Next time you see me, I'll be the queen of Monrock. You better start giving me some respect."

Ranvir could not believe what he just heard. Agatha just admitted her true colors and her intentions. Cecila was right about everything, and the fact he called her jealous made the whole situation worse. He lost his best friend over something she was trying to warn him about, but he didn't listen. He had his blinders on. Ranvir's heart hurt worse than the pain he was experiencing from the rose. He crawled back into bed, and tears started pouring down his cheeks. Ranvir started to grow weaker and weaker because of all the emotions he was having. He couldn't control them knowing that he lost his best friend over his stupidity and that his girlfriend was only using him for the throne and never loved him. The more Ranvir cried, the more pain he experienced. His energy was draining right from underneath him.

Chapter 11

Ranvir's energy started to drain fast. He wished he could've unheard the conversation he heard between Agatha and her friend Ameila. To hear Agatha say that she never loved Ranvir was such a huge act of betrayal for him. He trusted and believed in her, but he was let down and on the edge of death.

Elenor still had no luck in finding a cure. She knew she had to act fast because Ranvir was running out of time. If she didn't act soon, Ranvir would soon be a goner just like the rest of the victims.

"Anything, Elenor?" Mangus asked.

"I'm afraid not, Mangus. I will keep trying, but all you can do at this point is continue to make sure he is saving his energy as much as he can," Elenor said.

"So about the wedding, are we good to have it tomorrow?" Agatha asked.

"I guess so, but be careful with how you do it. A simple kiss could kill him instantly, but he seems to be doing all right."

"Good to hear! Make the announcement, Mangus," Agatha said.

"No need to rush, Agatha. I'll get around to it," Mangus said.

Agatha couldn't help but smile. She was soon about to become the queen. As long as Ranvir could stay alive a little longer by the time the ceremony was over, she knew there was nothing that could stop her.

Meanwhile, as Ranvir continued to lie in bed, he knew that Cecila would disown him as her friend after calling her jealous when she was right about Agatha all along. Ranvir knew he had to tell her. He rang the emergency bell and requested to see Cecila. A few minutes passed, and Cecila came into his room.

"Hey," Cecila said.

"Hey," Ranvir said weakly.

"How are you feeling? Have you been doing OK?"

"Not really."

"Is the pain getting worse?"

"It's been getting worse."

"Have you taken Elenor's potion at all today?"

"It's not the pain from the rose."

"What do you mean?"

Ranvir tried so hard to hold back his tears, but some became visible. He could already expect that Cecila was going to say, "I told you so."

"You were right," Ranvir said.

"About what?" Cecila asked.

Ranvir took a deep breath. He couldn't get any words out. Cecila knew that what he had to say wasn't good.

"Take a moment, Ranvir. Don't get yourself all worked up over it. I'm sure whatever it is that it'll be all right."

"You were right. You were right about Agatha."

Cecila was surprised, but she was not shocked. She knew eventually that he would find out the truth about Agatha.

"Hmm, was I now?" Cecila said.

"Go ahead! Say 'I told you so.' You tried to tell me, but I didn't listen. I was so blinded by love that it didn't run through my mind at all. So just go ahead and own it already. She didn't even have the audacity to say it to me in person. I had to find out through my own window when she was talking to Ameila," Ranvir said.

Cecila was shocked to hear that. She thought that Agatha would at least have some nerve to tell Ranvir in person. The fact that Ranvir heard it from outside his window made her heart hurt for him. As much as she wanted to tell Ranvir off, she knew as his best friend that she needed to be there for him.

"Ranvir, I don't know what to say. I'm so sorry that you had to hear it that way."

Ranvir was thrown off guard by her response. He expected Cecila to say "I told you so" and defend herself, but she didn't. Instead, she felt pity for him. He never expected her to do that after calling her jealous.

"What?"

"I'm so sorry you had to hear her say it outside your window. I can't even imagine what you're feeling right now."

"Horrible. I feel so betrayed."

"You have every right to be."

"Cecila, why are you agreeing and having pity for me? Shouldn't you be gloating at the fact you were right all this time? Aren't you mad that I called you jealous?"

"Well, one thing, you're my best friend. Of course, I'm going to have pity for you. I hate seeing you hurt."

"You still consider me as your friend? Despite what I said to you?"

"Ranvir, of course! I mean, I can understand why. I myself probably would've done the same thing too."

"I just feel like I'm back to square one now. I feel like I can't be king now knowing that Agatha wasn't here for the right reason."

"Well, yes, that's true that you're back to square one, but that doesn't mean your status of becoming king has to change."

"Yes, it does! There is no way I can do this by myself."

"Ranvir, you have been my best friend for a long time. I already saw you as a great king when I was young. I was the first one to see you as king and to believe in you. I watched you all this time asking yourself the same question for many years. There is something I never told you, but I wish I could've a long time ago. You are a strong and independent person. You always have been! You just never saw it for yourself. You just let Agatha take control of that. Even when you were with her, you were still that strong and independent person. You just didn't see it because—"

"I was so busy and put all my time into Agatha."

"Correct. Agatha just made it seem that way, but it wasn't the case all along. I mean, yes, you still had some doubts, but you never once took a step down. The only time you did was when she left you, but that was because she made it seem like you couldn't do it on your own. You have always been very powerful from the beginning. I know you can become the best king of all and rule the kingdom without anyone by your side. You don't need a queen by your side to prove yourself worthy of running a kingdom. You will be a great king, Ranvir, but you need to tell yourself that. That's the only way you'll feel more confident about yourself. Like I said, I already saw you as a powerful king from the beginning, and you always will."

Ranvir was taken aback by Cecila's words. Knowing that she still cared about him had a great impact, but what moved him the most was the fact she was right about himself being powerful on his own. It took him a second to figure it out, but as he took a trip down memory lane, he realized that Cecila was right. He had the independence and confidence all this time, but after Agatha left him, that's when he stopped believing in himself. Because of him not believing in himself, that's when he started to have doubts. It also explained the fact that he never got to see who the queen was that the rose showed to be. He thought it was a sign that he wasn't supposed to be with a queen right away and that he was supposed to rule the kingdom independently for a while.

"Cecila, I can't believe I'm saying this, but you're right. I can't believe that I didn't think about that before."

"And it's OK if you didn't figure it out until now, but from being your friend and being there for you all this time, I knew exactly what was happening because I was there for you every step of the way."

Cecila's words had a real impact on Ranvir. It made him realize that all this time, he was leaning toward the wrong person all his life. Cecila has been there for him every step of the way in his life, while Agatha left him without a reasonable explanation. She was there for him through the big and the small things that happened in his life. Ranvir suddenly came to the conclusion that he was with the wrong person. He should have been with Cecila instead of Agatha. Ranvir smiled really hard, finally figuring out everything. He ceased this moment to tell Cecila how he felt.

"Cecila, I was with the wrong person the entire time."

"And you now just figured that out?" she teased.

"I should've—"

Ranvir suddenly had another pain shoot from his side. The pain was so intense that he fell to the floor in pain. He started to become weaker. Cecila tried to help him up, but she could not physically do so.

"Mangus! Elenor!" Cecila shouted.

She ran to seek help from the both of them. Ranvir's life was now on the line. Any sudden movement could cause Ranvir to fall over, and his death would be right around the corner. Mangus and Elenor came into the room. Cecila stayed out of the room so she wouldn't risk his energy even further. Mangus helped him back into bed, while Elenor gave him another dose of the potion for the pain. Elenor knew his time was starting to run out more quickly.

"His time is almost up, Mangus. I will still try and do everything that I can. We need to be careful now. Anything could cause him to fall over and die any second now."

"He's gonna have to be isolated from everyone at this point. Nobody will be allowed to see him at this point forward, including Agatha. We're going to have to cancel the wedding. We're not going to be able to go through with it. Seeing Agatha could suck his energy out of him."

"No," Ranvir said weakly.

Mangus misinterpreted what Ranvir meant by no. He thought he still wanted to go through with the wedding, but Ranvir wanted to call it off completely now knowing Agatha's intentions.

"We'll figure out a way to make it work," Mangus said.

Ranvir could not get another word out. He wanted to tell him to call off the wedding, but he could not get any words out.

"Don't worry, son. It will work out."

"I'll continue to find something else to keep him alive longer and save his energy. I don't know how I'm going to find a cure with him getting worse."

"Please don't stop trying, Elenor."

"I'll do my best."

Mangus and Elenor both left the room. Mangus made his way to the front of the kingdom to tell everyone what was happening.

"My people, my son, Ranvir, is sadly not getting better. He is becoming weaker as we speak. I don't know how much time he has on his plate. I have come to make the decision that no one will be allowed to see him now. Anything could kill him at this point. As far as the wedding goes, we're going to have to figure something out. We may just have to do it without Ranvir's presence. It's the least we can do for Agatha," Mangus said.

"If I can just marry him, that'll be good enough for me. I just want to marry the love of my life," Agatha said.

"We'll figure something out," Mangus said.

"Soon I'll be the queen and everything will be OK," Agatha said.

"Not so fast, Agatha," Cecila said.

Chapter 12

Agatha turned around slowly to see who was talking to her. She couldn't help but laugh at the fact it was Cecila. She started to shake her head and made her way toward her.

"Cecila? What a pleasant surprise? I knew you would come around to talk to me," Agatha said.

"That's it? That's all you have to say to me?" Cecila said.

"Oh, I'm sorry, what would you like me to say?"

"How about I made a mistake? A really big one!"

"A mistake? Oh, you mean leaving Ranvir a year ago. It's OK. We talked about it already. I would've assumed that he told you. Did he not?"

"Oh, he did, all right! But not in the way I would've liked to hear! You clearly have issues!"

"What seems to be the issue, my dear? I thought I was fine the last time I checked, but I'll be glad to talk about it with you if you do see an issue."

"Don't 'my dear' me."

"My apologies. What would you like to be called, then?"

"Just Cecila."

"OK. What seems to be the issue, Cecila?"

"Stop playing this silly game, Agatha. I know what you're up to."

"About to marry your best friend? Yes. Isn't that what you wanted? Aren't you happy for him?"

"I was until I found out you were here for the wrong reason."

Everyone stood in shock. Agatha herself was even stumped. She turned around slowly to face Cecila.

"Wrong reason? What made you think that? I truly love Ranvir. I was with him for six years after all. Yes, I left for a year, but I'm not going anywhere. I promised him that."

"How do you even live with yourself? Just keep lying, Agatha."

The kingdom started to become confused. They had no idea what was going on. Mangus started to become confused himself.

"Lying? What do you mean, Cecila?" Mangus asked.

"Agatha was here for the wrong reason. She is only using Ranvir for the throne. She never loved him. I heard her say it herself. She is nothing but a liar!"

"A liar? Not at all. I don't know what has gotten into you. Are you just upset that I'm getting married and you're not? No need to feel jealous, Cecila."

"Jealous! Oh, you wish! I could never be jealous of someone who is using my friend! If anything, I feel sorry for you! I'm sorry that the truth has been revealed!"

Everyone started to whisper. They didn't know whom to believe. Cecila was getting very frustrated.

"Just keep running your mouth, Cecila. Haters are going to hate. Seems like you're the only one. Just let me go on and be happy with Ranvir."

"Agatha, quit lying! I heard you talking to your friend Ameila about it! That's right! I heard you. Why else would I bring this up? To make matters worse, Ranvir heard you!"

"Oh, please! Why would I dare put my future husband through that?"

"Hmm, maybe the fact you didn't have the guts to say it to his face. Also, maybe you weren't aware you were standing outside his window."

Agatha froze. She couldn't get any words out. She knew she was in a pickle at this point with no way out.

"He was so distraught when he heard you outside his window. You didn't have the guts to tell him yourself! You truly have no heart. You hurt Ranvir when you left! I was there and watched him hurt! You only came back because you knew he was about to become king. You should've just stayed gone. Ranvir is on the edge of his deathbed because of you! He loved you with all his heart, and you broke it into a million pieces. Why don't you just admit it already?"

"Keep running your mouth, Cecila. Nobody believes you! Do you really think they are going to listen to you over the future queen? I think not!"

"I believe her!" Ameila said.

Agatha turned around in anger. She couldn't believe that her own best friend would turn against her like that.

"What!"

"I said I believe her! I told you to tell Ranvir the truth all this time, but you refused to listen to me. You kept saying that nobody would find out. What'd I tell you? It's sick what you did."

"Oh, stop trying to defend Cecila. Don't feel bad for her. Besides, you're supposed to be my best friend, not hers!"

"I feel ashamed of calling you my best friend, especially that you're lying about it. Just fess up already. Cecila heard you, I heard you, and even Ranvir heard you. I warned you that this might happen. Welcome to reality. It sure stings, Agatha, doesn't it? How can you even consider marrying him if all you want out of it is to be queen? Oh, that's right, because you're using him! People of Monrock, Agatha never loved Ranvir. She was only using him!" Ameila said.

Everyone was in disbelief. Never would they have thought this about Agatha. Mangus was in absolute rage. Agatha didn't have anything to say.

"Agatha, I can't believe you. I thought you were the one for my son! I can't believe you would do this to me! Now my son could die any second because of your selfishness! You're a fool! You have no place to be queen," Mangus said.

"Face it, Agatha. You're a user! You were never in it for the right reason! All you cared about was your fame. You truly hurt Ranvir. You have nobody to blame but yourself at this point. Ranvir doesn't deserve you! You don't deserve him! Nobody deserves you! Why don't you do the whole kingdom a favor and just disappear like you did a year ago? Everything will be better once you're gone!" Cecila said.

The kingdom started to agree. Agatha was completely raged at this point. She reached her boiling point. She screamed at the top of her lungs, which frightened the entire kingdom.

"Oh, please. You really think I'm scared of—" Cecila said.

Agatha attempted to throw her shoe at her, but Cecila ducked. Agatha made a beeline straight toward her and started to choke her. Mangus managed to pull her off of Cecila, but Agatha elbowed him. Mangus's soldiers came and grabbed hold of Agatha.

"Call off your men, Mangus!" Agatha shouted.

"Never!" Mangus said.

"I SAID CALL THEM OFF!" Agatha screamed.

"It's OK, Mangus. If she wants to settle this like women, so be it. I'm not afraid of her! Let's duel this out like ladies!" Cecila said.

"Are you sure?" Mangus said.

"If that's what Agatha wants!"

"Oh, you already know it!" Agatha said.

Mangus's soldiers let her go. Cecila didn't know what she was about to get herself into, but she knew she needed to teach Agatha a lesson for using and hurting her best friend. Agatha pulled her hair up. She was ready to take Cecila down.

"We'll be over here in case this fight gets out of hand," Mangus said.

"I appreciate it, Mangus, but this is my own fight. I'm willing to do whatever it takes to protect my best friend!" Cecila said.

"Ranvir is lucky to have a great friend like you!" Mangus said.

Agatha felt disgusted by Cecila and her words. The two walked up toward each other in a preparation to fight one another.

"Bring it on, Agatha. You want to hurt my friend, you have to go through me first," Cecila said.

"As you wish!" Agatha said.

She charged straight toward Cecila, and they started to fight. The fighting was so intense that hair pulling and scratching were involved. Ranvir woke up from all the commotion. He had no idea what was going on. He slowly got out of bed and dragged himself toward the window. When he got to the window, he could not believe his eyes. He saw Agatha and Cecila fighting. Agatha was really giving it to Cecila.

"Cecila, Agatha, stop," Ranvir said weakly.

Ranvir knew he had to put an end to this. He needed to get to Cecila before Agatha could really harm her. He slowly made his way down the stairs. His energy was getting very low, but he was willing to give up the rest of his energy for the safety of his best friend.

"Just give up, Agatha! It's over! You have nowhere to go!" Cecila said.

"Says who!" Agatha said.

"Me!"

"You're nobody, Cecila!"

"You're talking to the wrong person, Agatha! I am more than you will ever be!"

"You were no one from the start—you never were!"

"I think you have your facts mixed up! You were no one before you got with Ranvir! You were just a sad young girl and played the victim until you met him. Now you are doing it again because everyone knows the truth now. You put that on yourself. You should have just stayed away. That would've been the right thing to do. You will never find anyone else like Ranvir again!"

Agatha was completely outraged at this point and flipped Cecila over her shoulder and slammed her to the ground. Cecila tried to get up but did the next best thing and used her foot to make Agatha fall. Cecila got up and started to walk away.

"Game over, Agatha! You need to leave!"

As Cecila walked away, Agatha threw a rock toward her to gain her attention. Cecila looked over at Agatha, who was now standing. Agatha reached for something under her belt. She pulled out a sword. Cecila froze. Ranvir made it out of the castle and saw this.

"Cecila," he said weakly.

He decided to use up all the energy he had left in him to save Cecila and to put a stop to Agatha. He started to run toward them.

"If I can't have Ranvir, NOBODY CAN!" Agatha shouted.

Agatha threw the sword sideways at Cecila. Ranvir ran as fast he could, using all the energy he had left in him.

"No!" Ranvir shouted.

Ranvir leaped and put himself in front of Cecila to protect her. The sword hit Ranvir in his side instead of Cecila. Agatha and Cecila suddenly realized what had happened.

"Ranvir!" they both said.

Chapter 13

They both ran to Ranvir's side. Ranvir could hardly breathe. The sword hitting him was the final thing that caused all his energy to drain out.

"Get away from him," Cecila said.

"No, you!" Agatha said.

"You've done enough! Get away from Ranvir!"

"Not as long as I'm standing here!"

"Agatha, st-stop. You need to get aw-away," Ranvir said weakly.

Mangus and everyone saw what was going on and immediately ran toward Ranvir. They had no idea what they were about to get themselves into. Mangus was at a loss for words seeing his son like this.

"Ranvir! Oh, no! No! What's happening!" Mangus said.

"Agatha threw a sword, and it hit Ranvir. I think he's out of time," Cecila said.

"No, you don't understand. He got in the way!" Agatha said.

"Guards!" Mangus said.

"No, I'm innocent, I tell you! Innocent!" Agatha shouted.

"Silence!" one guard said.

"I don't wanna hear another word out of your mouth!" another said.

The guards grabbed Agatha and put her hands behind her back. They held her in contempt so she would not slip away.

"Get your hands off me!" Agatha said.

She tried to kick them to let her free, but they stood their ground and waited for Mangus to give the order. Mangus supported Ranvir's head to take the pressure off his wound and the sword.

"Ranvir! Ranvir! Son, can you hear me!" Mangus said.

Ranvir moaned in pain. He could not speak. The pain was unbearable at this point. He felt his time was now coming to an end. He fought to stay alive. Elenor ran to Ranvir as fast as she could. She got to her knees and gave her the potion for the pain and was trying to heal his wound. Ranvir hissed in pain.

"I know, Ranvir. I'm trying to save your energy," Elenor said.

"Please try to save him!" Mangus cried.

"Please," Cecila said.

"I'm trying. I just don't—" Elenor said.

"Elenor," Ranvir said weakly.

"Yes, Ranvir?" Elenor said.

"I can't feel my toes," Ranvir said weakly.

Elenor froze. She knew exactly what that meant. She tried to hold a straight face for everyone, but she felt tears coming on.

"Elenor, what is it?" Mangus asked.

"I'm so sorry, Mangus. Ranvir is fading away," Elenor said.

Mangus froze too. He looked at his son and saw his body slowly fading away starting with his feet. Tears started to build up in his eyes.

"He can't be," Mangus said.

"I'm so sorry," Elenor said.

"Elenor, please, you have to do something!" Mangus cried.

"I'm sorry, Mangus. There is nothing more I can do. He must have used up all that energy when coming out from the castle and taking the sword for Cecila. Like I told you, a simple kiss could have killed him, but it seems like the sword did. Once the victim's energy has completely drained, their body starts to fade. Now's your time to say your good-byes. I'm so sorry, Mangus. I wish there was something that I could do, but I don't know the cure."

Mangus could not hold back his tears. He had to face the fact that he was losing his son. He was now going to lose everyone in his family whom he loved. He felt like a failure because there was nothing he could do to save Ranvir.

Ranvir could feel himself fading away. He knew his time was up. He knew he had to say something before he could never say it again.

"Dad," Ranvir said weakly.

"Yes, bud? I'm right here," Mangus said.

"I'm-I'm sorry."

"No, Ranvir. I'm sorry. It's my fault. I should have never pressured you into becoming king so early."

"No. It's my fault. I'm the one who sought the rose in the first place. I was so selfish. I thought I couldn't do anything without a queen, but the truth is I don't. I wish I could've seen that sooner."

"I understand where you came from, though. I won't lie. It was tough doing it on my own when your mother and sister passed. Now you'll be able to be with them. I thought I was going to see them first, but looks like you beat me to it. Please say hi to them for me."

"I will."

"You would've been a great king," Mangus said.

"I know. I just wish I could've figured that all out sooner. More so, I wish I was with the right person. I know what I want now, but, sadly, it's too late to fix it. I'm sorry that I won't become king. I want Cecila to become queen. It was she I should've been with all along," Ranvir said weakly.

Cecila heard and couldn't help but get emotional. Knowing that Ranvir should've been with her made her realize that they could've been something special. Now they couldn't because Ranvir was dying. Ranvir's body was now fading a lot quicker.

"Cecila," Ranvir said weakly.

"Yes?" Cecila.

Ranvir held out his hand to her. She held it briefly. Her tears started to become uncontrollable.

"I wish . . . I wish . . . I wish it was you. Be the next queen for me. My people need you. I wouldn't want anyone else to do it but you. Take good care of our people for me."

"I will, Ranvir," Cecila said.

Ranvir's body had almost faded away. Everyone in the kingdom started to get emotional knowing that they were about to lose their prince. Everyone gathered around Ranvir and joined hands in honor of his last moments before he faded away for good.

"I'm starting to see light," Ranvir said weakly.

Mangus's tears could not be controlled. He never thought he would have to say good-bye to his son. If anything, he thought Ranvir would be the one to bury him, but it was the other way around.

"I love you so much, son! My precious boy, I never thought this day would come, but I know you'll be a great king up there with your mom and sister. You'll get to see them again. Tell them both that I love them and I'll see them when my day comes," Mangus said.

"I will. I love you too," Ranvir said weakly.

Mangus managed to hug what was left of Ranvir. He held him so tight, he didn't want to let him go. He pulled away to see his son about to fade away any second now. Ranvir looked over at Cecila.

"I should've been with . . .." Ranvir said weakly.

Ranvir didn't have time to finish his sentence. Ranvir's body completely faded away. He disappeared. Ranvir was gone. Everyone was in tears.

"Ranvir is gone. He's dead," Elenor said.

Everyone started to grieve over Ranvir's death. Mangus ordered his men to lock up Agatha in the cell until further notice. Mangus was now in a dark place with the loss of his son. Everyone comforted him with everything they had in them. Elenor gathered everyone around the garden to honor Prince Ranvir.

"My lord, we gather here today in the garden for the loss of our beloved prince Ranvir, the son of King Mangus and Queen Regina, and the brother of Princess Reya. May you reunite the three of them together again. We ask for a healing to everyone in the kingdom as they have suffered a great loss. Altogether, we lost a warrior, a fighter, a prince, a leader, a brother, a son, a friend. Keep his memory alive for us all," Elenor said.

Everyone held hands and came together as one. This was déjà vu for Mangus. He had to go through this with his wife and daughter, and now it was his son.

"Cecila, I want you to honor Ranvir. If anyone has the power to do so, it's you," Mangus said.

"Thank you, Mangus!" Cecila said.

Cecila stood in front of everyone. She tried to hold back her tears but let out a few. She got herself together and started to speak.

"People of Monrock, Prince Ranvir was a strong and independent man. He would stop at nothing to make others happy. Although he had some doubts in the beginning of taking his place, he soon found it in his heart to realize he didn't need anyone to be successful. He always put others before himself. He gave the last bit of his energy to save me from being stabbed. Rather than staying in his bed and saving his energy to stay alive, he sacrificed himself so I wouldn't get hurt. If that isn't what an act of bravery is, I don't know what is. Ranvir was a warrior and will always be. He gave me the task to take over for Mangus and take my place as queen. As much as I am thrilled, I can't. This was meant to be for Ranvir, but I am willing to step in for Monrock to make sure they have a leader. But it should've been Ranvir. I made him a promise, and I am sticking to it," Cecila said.

Everyone clapped. Cecila went over to Mangus and hugged him. She cried on his shoulder.

"He would be so proud of you right now," Mangus said.

"Thank you," Cecila said.

Elenor suddenly felt something, something she never felt before. She knew something was happening.

"Mangus, did you feel something?" Elenor said.

"Feel what?" Mangus said.

"Like this feeling of magic."

"No."

"I feel something happening. Last time I got this feeling, it was good. Something is happening, and it's a good thing."

As soon as she said those words, everyone started to feel it too. They started to see this light of magic into the garden. Nobody knew what it was. They were frightened at first, but Elenor reassured them that there was nothing to fear. They couldn't stop staring at the wisp of magic. Elenor smiled.

"I think I finally figured out what the cure is," Elenor said.

Chapter 14

The magic kept growing all around the garden. Everyone couldn't take their eyes off of it. A huge burst of magic suddenly exploded. Everyone covered their eyes because of the brightness. The magic started to slow down and made a transformation of a body. The magic soon disappeared, and it was revealed to be Ranvir. Ranvir was brought back to life. He looked better than ever before he came into contact with the rose. It's like a new Ranvir was born. His skin was healthier, his blond hair was brighter and smoother, and his smile was shiny as the sun. Elenor smiled as she knew it was he all along. Nobody could believe what their eyes were seeing. Was Ranvir really alive, or was it their imagination?

"Ranvir?" Mangus said.

"Hey, Dad," Ranvir said.

Mangus made a beeline straight toward him. He pulled him straight into a hug. Mangus started to cry knowing that his son came back to life. He never wanted to let him go. Ranvir hugged him back harder.

"Oh my gosh, you're alive!" Mangus cried.

"I am, Dad, and I'm not going anywhere again. I made a promise to be the best king I could be, and I intend to keep it that way," Ranvir said.

"I love you so much, son!" Mangus said.

"I love you too!" Ranvir said.

"Ranvir!" Cecila said.

"Cecila."

Cecila hugged him. She still couldn't believe her eyes. One moment, Ranvir was gone, but now he was back. The rest of the people came up to Ranvir and hugged him. They all rejoiced in his reappearance.

"Elenor, I thought you said there was no cure for the rose. How was I brought back to life?" Ranvir said.

"You found the cure, Ranvir. You brought yourself back to life," Elenor said.

"How? What was it?" Ranvir asked.

"Sacrifice," Elenor said.

Everyone looked at each other weird. They had no idea how sacrifice could bring someone back to life.

"Really? How?" Ranvir said.

"Well, you see, I've seen that magic before. It means that someone is being brought back to life. Once I saw the magic bringing you back, it all made sense once I added the pieces of the puzzle together," Elenor said.

"I'm listening," Ranvir said.

"Well, as you know, the rose came with consequences. Since you decided to take that risk, you sacrificed yourself to know what your fate was. When your body was giving out and you knew that your friend was in trouble, you sacrificed your remaining energy and yourself to save the one that you loved. You were willing to give your life to save Cecila from being stabbed. Once Cecila mentioned it in the garden, that's when I knew. You have unlocked the mystery I've been looking for, for a long time. Not only are you the future king of Monrock, but also you're a hero. Now, millions of lives can be saved now that I know what the cure is to get rid of the rose once and for all. Thank you, Ranvir!" Elenor said.

"I'm glad to be the one to find it!" Ranvir said.

"Wait, Elenor, you said 'the one that you loved'? Ranvir, you love me?" Cecila said.

Ranvir smiled really hard. He started to blush. He could now tell Cecila how he felt without any other interruptions.

"Cecila, you have been my best friend since the beginning. All my life, I was leaning toward the wrong person. I should've been with you all my life instead of Agatha. After you told me that I was a strong and independent person, that's when I realized it. You were there for me through the hard times, and I always had you to lean on. I wish I would've seen it sooner, but better now than never. I know that's somebody I want by my side. If I could choose someone else to be with, it would be you. I want to be with you. I love you! Will you be my girlfriend?" Ranvir said.

Everyone couldn't help but show emotion to how sweet it was seeing Ranvir open up to Cecila. Cecila could not hold back any longer. She knew this day would come, and Ranvir finally asked the question.

"Yes! Yes, of course, I will. What took you so long to ask!" Cecila said.

Ranvir smiled and hugged her. He was about to kiss her, but he saw the guards chasing Agatha.

"Stop her! She escaped from her cell!" one shouted.

"Leave her, gentlemen. I have words to say," Ranvir said.

"As you wish, my king," one said.

"Ranvir! How is that possible! I saw your body fade away," Agatha said.

"Surprise," Ranvir said.

"I'm so confused," Agatha said.

"Turns out sacrifice is the cure to the rose," Ranvir said.

"So you're alive?"

"That's right, and better than ever. No more pain. Everything is healed now, especially the wound from where you threw the sword."

"Ranvir, you know I didn't mean to throw the sword at you. It was meant for Cecila."

"I'm quite aware of that." He held Cecila's hand.

"Oh, thank good— Wait! You two are together now?" Agatha said.

"Yes. She was the one whom I should've been with all my life, not you. You never cared about me at all. You left me high and dry for a year and to only come back so you can become queen."

"Ranvir, I already told you how sorry I was about that."

"But were you, though? Or is that what you were trying to say for me to take you back? Just admit it, Agatha, you were never here for the right reason. I heard every word you said outside my window, Agatha, all of it. You hurt me. It's ironic because you literally did stab me."

"That was an accident."

"Yes, I know, but was it an accident when you were using me? I don't think so."

"Using you? Why do you think that I was using you? If anything, I truly loved you with everything that I had."

"You know that's not true. Otherwise, you would have never told Ameila outside my window. She's smarter than you. You should've never come back at all. All the times when I thought I needed a queen and someone by my side to be successful in ruling an entire kingdom, I was wrong. Cecila is the one who made me realize that, and I'm thankful that I realized it now rather than having to be fooled into a marriage with you. It also made me realize that she has been there for me since the beginning and I was with the wrong person all my life. You were never here for the right reason, so you deserve no purpose of being here any longer."

"What are you saying?"

"First of all, I forgive you, Agatha."

Everyone was shocked to hear that. They knew there had to be a catch somewhere. Cecila looked at Ranvir but gave her the look as he knew what he was about to say.

"Really? Oh, what a relief!" Agatha said.

"Hold on. Don't get too comfortable now. I wasn't finished."

"OK. What is it?"

"Like I said, you have no purpose of being here anymore after knowing your true intentions. As the future king, you are banished from the kingdom for good."

Agatha's jaw dropped to the ground. She couldn't believe what Ranvir said. Everyone couldn't help but laugh.

"What! You can't do that! You are no king yet!"

"Oh, yes, I can. I have more power than you will ever have. You should have never messed with me in the beginning. You should've just stayed gone. Have her on the next ship out, my soldiers."

"Yes, sir!" one said.

"Mom! Say something! Guys, say something! Tell them not to take me away," Agatha said.

Agatha's mom and brothers had no words for her. They just stood there. They knew that Agatha needed to learn a lesson for being selfish, so they thought her being banished was a good thing, especially because they were hurt when Agatha left them behind for a year as well.

"I think this is good for you. Now you will understand the emotions we went through when you left us like you did to Ranvir. Let this be a lesson to you, Agatha. Good luck on your own! I'm sure you'll survive," her mother said.

"No! No! Tell them to let me go," Agatha said.

The guards grabbed hold of Agatha's arms. People started to clap knowing that they won't have to see Agatha again. They placed her on the ship and sailed her off somewhere far off from Monrock.

"It is done, my king. You will not be seeing her for a long time," one soldier said.

"Excellent. I have all that I need right here," Ranvir said.

Later on in the day, Ranvir and Mangus had some time to talk things over. Mangus knew he would never take Ranvir for granted again.

"So did you end up seeing your mom and sister?" Mangus asked.

"I did actually," Ranvir said.

"Really? Did they look any different?"

"Mom, no. But Reya, yes, obviously because she would've been twenty-five if she were still here. She looked like Mom, though."

"I bet she does. You take after your mom a little bit too."

"Yeah. It was great to see them again. At first, I was over the moon to be reunited with them again, but they knew it wasn't my time yet."

"What do you mean?"

"They told me that I needed to go back and be the king that I desired to be. They told me they were super proud of me, and the next thing I knew, I was back. It all happened so fast."

"And now you're a hero. You discovered the cure to the fate-rose. Now nobody can find it again."

"I'm glad to be the one to have figured that out."

"So I wanted to ask you something."

"Sure. Anything."

"About this whole becoming king early, I'm really sorry if I tried to push it so early. It's your choice. You don't have to become king now. If you wish to wait until your coming of age comes, I will support whatever you decide."

"Well, after realizing what Cecila told me, I'm more ready than ever to be king. I want to become king now because I want to, not because I have Cecila as my girlfriend."

"Do you think she'll be your queen one day?"

"Hopefully, but after learning from my mistake, I'm not going to rush into it. If it happens, it'll happen. I'm going to take it one day at a time."

"That's my son! I knew you would come around the idea. When do you want to have the coronation?"

"Maybe next week?"

'Really? So soon? I like the sound of that. You got it, son. Monrock will be happy to have you as their new king."

"Thanks, Dad!"

Chapter 15

Today was the day. Ranvir was finally becoming king. He could barely sleep that night having all the excitement running through his mind. He looked in the mirror and saw himself as the king he always knew he could be. Today was the day he was about to make his father proud. There was a knock on the door.

"It's open," Ranvir said.

Mangus came in. He couldn't help but smile. He thought he was looking at a younger version of himself when he became king.

"You look just like me on my big day," Mangus said.

"Do I?" Ranvir said.

"Of course."

"I can't believe it's actually happening. A week ago, I thought I would never get to this point, but now here I am striving to make my people happy."

"I'm happy to hear that, son."

"I couldn't sleep last night. I had all these jitters running through my head."

"Are you nervous? It's OK to be. I will never forget how nervous I was. I almost didn't walk down the aisle, but I knew I needed to take my place."

"Kinda, but I'm excited. This is a new chapter for me, and I'm excited to see what it has in store."

"Being king is a huge responsibility, but if anyone can do it, it's you.

You and I have the power to do anything as long as we believe. Yes, we may have had to go through a horrible experience to realize it, but it's what makes us stronger."

"Thanks, Dad!"

"I wanted to bring this up. Normally, it's a tradition for the new king to have a first dance with their mother, but I figured you would have it with Cecila."

"Most definitely. I should've danced with her that night instead of . . . you know."

"True, but again, everything happens for a reason. Now you found your happily ever after. Now you can make your dream a reality."

"Yep. I'm ready to start this new life."

"I'm proud of you, son. The people of Monrock are blessed to call you their king."

"Ranvir?" Cecila said.

Cecila was standing at the foot of the door. Ranvir smiled seeing her all dressed up and beautiful.

"Speaking of your girl! I'll give you both a moment. See you down there, Ranvir," Mangus teased.

Mangus left the room. Ranvir smiled really hard. He never thought he and Cecila would be together. It was like he escaped a great danger and found what he was looking for all his life.

"Did you get all dressed up for me?" Ranvir asked.

"Of course, babe! It's your special day," Cecila said.

"Well, it wouldn't have been if it wasn't for you."

"Aw, now, are you going to try and make me cry my makeup off before the coronation starts?"

"I'll try not to."

"Well, I just wanted to come by and see you before. I'll see you downstairs. I'm super proud of you!"

Before Cecila could leave, Ranvir grabbed her hand. Cecila knew that he meant business when he would do something like that.

"Cecila, as you know, it's a tradition that the future king has the first dance with their mother. Well, you know I can't have that. So I was wondering if you will do the honor and do the first dance with me?"

"Ranvir, of course, I will!"

Ranvir hugged her. He once cared for Cecila as a friend, but now he could call her his girlfriend like he should've all this time. She kissed his cheek. Ranvir started to blush.

"I'll see you down there."

"I'll see you soon."

Cecila smiled and walked out of the room. Before Ranvir went down, he looked at a family portrait that he always passed when he walked in the castle. He put his hand on it.

"Today's the day, Mom and Reya. This day could not be any more special without thinking of you two. I know for a fact you're watching in the sky. I promise to be the best king of Monrock. That's what you both would have wanted. I'm thinking about you both," Ranvir said.

Ranvir made his way to the coronation room. He took a deep breath as he was about to walk through those doors. Standing by those doors happened to be the spirit of Regina and Reya. Ranvir had no idea if he was daydreaming or not, but he let out a few tears.

"Welcome to this day, my son. You have earned your rightful place as king. Go make your people proud," Regina said.

"Monrock is in good hands. Good luck today, brother. I'm always here if you need me. I always knew you would become the next heir," Reya said.

Ranvir tried to control his tears, but more slipped out. He hugged both Regina and Reya and felt them hug him back.

"I'm proud of you, my son! Take good care of the kingdom!"

"I love you, Mom and Reya!"

"We love you too!" Reya said.

"Always do what is best! You got this. You have always had the power to do so. We'll see you very soon! Take care of everyone for us," Regina said.

"I will!"

Regina and Reya's spirits disappeared. Ranvir felt more determined than ever after hearing his mom and sister's words.

"Ready, my lord?" a soldier said.

"Yes! Ready than ever!" Ranvir said.

The guards opened the doors. Ranvir walked down the aisle toward the front. Everyone stood before him. When he made it to the front, everyone remained seated.

"Your Highness, are you willing to take the oath to become king?" the bishop said.

"Yes, I am willing," Ranvir said.

"Do you promise to look after your people and protect them at all cost?"

"I promise," Ranvir said.

"Will you use your power as a king to bring law and justice if needed by your decisions and judgments?"

"I will," Ranvir said.

After taking many oaths, Ranvir was now about to be crowned. He got down on one knee. Mangus took a sword and placed it on each side gently. He then took off his crown and placed it on Ranvir's head.

"King Ranvir of Monrock!" Mangus said.

"King Ranvir of Monrock!" everyone said.

They all stood to their feet and clapped. Ranvir smiled really hard. He walked back down the aisle now as the king of Monrock. He could not be any happier. Later that evening, everyone gathered into the ballroom to celebrate. When Ranvir entered the room, everyone bowed before him.

"King Ranvir, everyone!" Mangus said.

Ranvir was about to give his speech. He felt butterflies. He looked over at Mangus, and he nodded to him, telling him that he's got this.

"People of Monrock, today is the day I took my place as king. I'm not going to lie. It was a tough choice for me to take. At first, I wasn't sure if I was cut out to be king, mostly because I thought I wasn't capable of running an entire kingdom all by myself. After the death of my mom and sister and having to see my dad go through it alone, it made me worry more that it could happen to me. I eventually found someone whom I thought would've been my queen, but after she did what she did to me, I didn't want to become king at all—all because I thought I couldn't be a successful ruler without someone by my side. It turns out I already had that. I just never saw it because I had my guard up and blinders on the entire time. All it took was for someone to tell me that I was a strong and independent person and that I was capable of doing anything to make me realize I was leaning toward the wrong person all my life. Knowing that, I knew I was more cut out to become king than what I would've thought. It turns out the fate-rose was right. It didn't tell me who my queen was—meaning that I don't need one to make me be a successful ruler, not now anyway. Encountering the rose changed my outlook on everything. Today, I am proud to stand tall and call you all my people. I am proud to be your king!" Ranvir said.

Everyone clapped. Cecila smiled really hard. Ranvir hugged Mangus while shedding a few tears.

"You did good, son. Now go make your people proud," Mangus said.

"As you know, it's a tradition that the king is supposed to have a first dance. Well, since my mom is not with us physically, I know for a fact she's here. I can feel her presence. Tonight, I will be doing my first dance with my girlfriend, Cecila, the one whom I should have been with all my life," Ranvir said.

Cecila smiled. She took his hand, and they started to dance. Everyone smiled really hard seeing Ranvir happy again. They knew he truly found his soul mate. After their first dance, everyone joined them on the dance floor for a slow dance. Ranvir had so many thoughts running through his mind. He was dancing with the girl of his dreams. He was in such a happy place.

"This brings me back to the night where I met her," Ranvir said.

"And that's a good thing because?" Cecila said.

"Meaning I should've asked you to dance that night instead of her."

"Well, now you have that! I'm not going anywhere."

"I love when you're reassuring!"

"I try to be."

"There's something I should've done a long time ago but never had the courage to do it as kids. Now that we're official . . ."

"What's that?"

Ranvir moved some of her hair from her eyes and started to move closer to her. He placed his hand on her cheek and gave her the most beautiful, passionate kiss that she has been waiting for. So much love and passion were put into the kiss. As they pulled away, they both smiled hard, and Cecila rested her head on his shoulder, and Ranvir continued to hold her close.

"I love you!" he whispered in her ear.

"I love you too," she whispered.

Everyone remained dancing and continued to celebrate Ranvir becoming king. Now that Elenor knew what the cure was, she was able to get rid of the rose once and for all. She no longer had to deal with any more cases.

Everyone has a fate. People may not know what it is, but to find out comes a sacrifice when knowing what exactly can happen. It may not come with consequences like the fate-rose did, but it can be scary to find out. Sometimes, people have to go through something they may not like to know what it is, but in the end, it is all worth it.